FUTURE PERFECT

ELISABETH LIDBETTER

WESTBOW
PRESS®
A DIVISION OF THOMAS NELSON
& ZONDERVAN

Scripture quotations are taken from The Holy Bible, New International
Version®, NIV® Copyright © 1973, 1978, 1984, 2011 by Biblica,
Inc.® Used by permission. All rights reserved worldwide.

This is a work of fiction. All of the characters, names, incidents,
organizations, and dialogue in this novel are either the products
of the author's imagination or are used fictitiously.

WestBow Press books may be ordered through booksellers or by contacting:

WestBow Press
A Division of Thomas Nelson & Zondervan
1663 Liberty Drive
Bloomington, IN 47403
www.westbowpress.com
1 (866) 928-1240

Because of the dynamic nature of the Internet, any web addresses or
links contained in this book may have changed since publication and
may no longer be valid. The views expressed in this work are solely those
of the author and do not necessarily reflect the views of the publisher,
and the publisher hereby disclaims any responsibility for them.

Any people depicted in stock imagery provided by Getty Images are models,
and such images are being used for illustrative purposes only.
Certain stock imagery © Getty Images.

ISBN: 978-1-9736-4529-0 (sc)
ISBN: 978-1-9736-4530-6 (e)

Print information available on the last page.

WestBow Press rev. date: 11/28/2018

CHAPTER 1

Emma felt suddenly that it was impossible to stay in the house any longer. She dressed the twins in their outdoor clothes with meticulous care and settled them into their double stroller, wrapping them up in their soft fleecy blankets. The familiarity of the oft-repeated process was calming; the trembling of her hands eased and her incipient tears receded as she dealt with the sweetly sleeping babies and checked through the contents of their changing bag.

Shrugging herself into a coat and picking up her purse and keys, she let herself out of the front door into the bright, blustery April morning, and began to walk, pushing the stroller before her, with no real thought as to where she was heading, only a desperate need to get out of the house and away from the thoughts and the memories that were pressing in on her.

The events of the last two days seemed to replay endlessly through her subconscious, surfacing as soon as she relaxed her guard. Her head felt as though it were filled with cotton wool, as though the mechanisms of thought were impeded by some obstruction. She barely noticed the neat streets of suburban houses with their clean paint and their tidy gardens as she trod along the pavements, heading steadily away from home, trying unavailingly to subdue the chaos inside her.

She walked through the local park, seeing but scarcely registering that very few people had braved the windy weather. There were two sturdy toddlers in the play area, their mothers, well wrapped up against the breeze, watched from a bench nearby, chatting desultorily while a few ducks bobbed on the pond behind them; a couple of brisk dog walkers were in evidence; and a frail, old gentleman tipped his hat to Emma as he tottered past with a newspaper under his arm, his eyesight too poor to be alarmed by her blank pallor.

She couldn't think what she should do with the day – with her life. She just couldn't think, couldn't even pray about any of the major issues she was facing.

Leaving the park by the far gate, she continued to walk – past a small parade of shops, shabby and dated, but still providing a useful service to the community, especially the elderly who could potter out for supplies and a chat with local shopkeepers to while away an empty morning. Emma did not need to stop for any supplies. Lately, her well-ordered life had included an efficiently planned, fortnightly delivery of shopping and the twins, Millie and Joel, were fully catered for as they had not yet progressed to solid food.

It crossed Emma's mind to wonder, in a distant kind of way, what her financial situation would be now. She supposed hazily that she would have to talk to a lawyer or to the bank, but she couldn't begin to think how the process would work nor what the outcome could possibly be. She had a brief, vivid memory of Sam telling her earnestly shortly after they had married that he kept all his important documents in the locked box-file under his desk and showing her where he kept the key – under the pen tray in the top drawer of the desk. She could plainly recall his serious expression, the tone of his voice, his square hands with their blunt fingers and neatly trimmed nails as he had lifted the tray to reveal the carefully concealed key. Her mind shied away from the memory and she walked on, pushing the stroller steadily further and further away from home, as half-formed images and thoughts flashed unbidden through her mind in random patterns.

A large raindrop landing on one knuckle recalled her to some awareness of her surroundings. Easing her tight grip on the handle of the pushchair, she looked up and saw that the boisterous April wind had blown up a scudding swirl of heavy, grey clouds. Deftly, she secured the hood of the stroller and fastened the plastic cover across the still sleeping twins. She noticed that Millie was beginning to stir and, glancing at her watch, realised that they would soon be hungry.

The rain began to fall more steadily and, by the time Emma had pulled up her own hood and tied it under her chin, it had become a downpour. She turned the pushchair to retrace her steps but as she did so she was calculating that they were at least half an hour's brisk walk from home and that they were likely to be soaked through long before they arrived. She sent up a brief prayer and, looking around, it dawned on her that she was only a few streets away from Charlotte's house. On impulse she set off in that direction. Charlie was a longstanding friend and had a toddler of her own - little Dan, Emma's godson. Charlie would understand;

she would welcome Emma in and give her a safe haven, somewhere to feed the twins and wait out the cloudburst.

Emma's feet slowed momentarily as she realised that she would not be able to avoid breaking the news of recent events to Charlie. She shrank from the idea but she knew she would have to tell people sooner or later and to be able to start with Charlie, who was one of her closest friends, must be counted a blessing.

As the ferocity of the rainstorm increased, Emma began to move faster, until she was almost running with the stroller over the uneven pavements. The cold drops struck her face and hands with stinging force and a tiny wail came from one of the twins, shortly followed by another. Soon a second voice had joined in and both babies were protesting in chorus.

All at once, it was too much for Emma. Salty tears mingled with the rain on her cheeks and she sobbed as she hurried down the street, turned the corner and headed like a hunted animal for the shelter of Charlie's house.

Her cold, wet fingers fumbled with the latch on the garden gate and then there was the usual problem of negotiating the gate with the unwieldy pushchair, while the rain fell unremittingly and the twins howled. It was with a sense of relief that Emma reached the shelter of the open porch. She clumsily untied her hood and pushed it down before reaching up to ring the doorbell.

"Just a minute now; just a minute," she soothed the twins, rocking the pushchair and waiting for the door to open. As the delay lengthened, she wondered for the first time what she would do if Charlie were out. No solution presented itself and, with a little prayer of desperation, she pressed the doorbell again. Almost immediately, over the wailing of the babies, she caught sounds of movement inside and the door opened.

Emma looked up thankfully to greet her friend, an explanation on the tip of her tongue, but found herself staring at a completely unexpected apparition. A tall, lean, dark-haired young man in jeans and a jumper – not Charlie's husband, Edward, who was solid and blond, but one of Ed's friends – in fact, someone Emma had not seen for six years and had thought never to see again.

"Nick!" she gasped, as the twins continued to protest.

He looked even more shaken than she felt and, of course, she presented a shocking enough picture: cold, dripping wet and with the marks of her distress visible in her face.

"Emma?" he exclaimed on a note of astonishment, his voice splitting on the disyllable.

"What are you doing here?" she demanded in accusatory tones.

He seemed to pull himself together with some difficulty. "I'm staying with Ed and Charlie."

"Is Charlie in?"

"No, she popped to the shops with Dan a little while ago."

Emma's face fell and her shoulders slumped in defeat.

"What's wrong?" Nick asked, but Emma only shook her head, close to tears once more.

"She'll be back soon, I expect," Nick offered reassuringly. "Come in out of the rain and wait."

As he spoke, he stooped and lifted the pushchair in over the threshold. Emma followed reluctantly. She really did not want to spend any time with Nick but she could not think of an alternative. Her fingers dealt automatically with the fastenings of her coat and she shed the soaked garment and went over to the twins, whose demands for attention were growing ever more persistent. Having removed the rain-cover from the stroller, she loosened the blankets, relieved to find that they were largely dry, and lifted Millie out. Her cries ceased at the awareness of movement and the prospect of attention, but Joel, left by himself in the pushchair, continued to advertise his hunger and annoyance in the traditional fashion.

"So these are your twins," Nick remarked in a carefully conversational tone. "Ed told me you'd acquired two for the price of one. Would you like a hand with this one?" He indicated towards Joel as he spoke.

"Well, er – if you don't mind," Emma stammered, unable to think of a sensible way of refusing his assistance in the face of Joel's squalling, but completely thrown by Nick's presence and the notion of his having anything to do with Sam's children.

"What are their names?" Nick asked, as he gently lifted the screaming Joel from the pushchair and cradled him against his broad shoulder.

"That's Joel," Emma said, with some reserve. "And this one's Mille; and I'm afraid they're both hungry."

She began to extract Millie from her snowsuit and Nick did the same for Joel.

"Come through to the sitting room," he suggested when they had finished, and led the way without waiting to see whether she would follow - although of course she did, as he was walking off with one of her babies.

Joel's protests had subsided and in the ensuing quietness Nick offered Emma a seat. "When Charlie gets back, I'll put the kettle on, but we've got our hands rather full at the moment," he said, with an uneasy smile.

He lowered himself carefully into an armchair as he spoke and Emma followed suit, but within a matter of seconds both babies had started crying again and the adults got resignedly back to their feet.

"My niece is just the same," Nick remarked. "I think babies are born with some kind of inbuilt sensor for immediate detection of dereliction of duty – it's obviously unacceptable to sit down on the job!"

"How old is your niece?" Emma asked, ignoring his attempt at humour.

"Well, I've got several but Sally, the youngest, is about seven months. And these two little bundles?"

"Eleven weeks."

"Are they sleeping through the night yet?" Nick enquired.

"Sometimes."

An awkward pause developed. To break it, Nick asked expressionlessly, "How's your husband?" He was transferring Joel from one shoulder to the other as he spoke and seemed to be concentrating studiously on the task in hand.

There was another pause, which lengthened into an appalling, oppressive silence as Emma's mind raced round in panic stricken circles, but it was impossible not to answer and eventually she said baldly and heavily, "He's dead."

"*Dead!*" Nick's voice cracked again and, through her own distress, Emma heard his sharp intake of breath.

She struggled for composure. She had cried so much in the last two days.

"Oh, my dear!" Nick said gently. "I am so sorry."

His sympathy undid her and the tears flowed unchecked down her cheeks.

Nick took a hesitant step towards her and then retreated, for there was no comfort he could offer.

At this juncture, sounds betokening an arrival were heard and Emma wiped her eyes with the back of one hand, sniffed and blinked in an attempt to regain some control, while Nick looked on in sombre concern and continued to rock baby Joel.

Within seconds, Charlotte had breezed into the room with little Dan in tow. Comfortably plump, with short, brown hair, a serene countenance and a warm smile, she was generally placid and good-tempered. Seeing Emma, she exclaimed cheerfully, "So it's *your* pushchair! I wondered why there was a double buggy in my hall. How lovely to see you! I'm sorry I was out - you should have let me know you were coming. I hope Nick has been looking after you…"

Her voice trailed away and she moved quickly to greet her friend, while Dan headed single-mindedly for his toy box. As Charlotte drew closer, she became aware of Emma's reddened nose and swimming eyes and, leaning forwards to kiss her warmly on the cheek, she asked with quick concern what was wrong.

Emma could not immediately speak through the tears which had begun to fall again, and Charlotte looked frowningly at Nick.

"She told me that Sam is dead," he clarified tersely.

"*Sam?* Sam *Barton?*" Charlotte asked in disbelief.

"Yes."

"But when -? How -?"

"I don't know anything more."

Charlotte turned back to Emma and put her arm comfortingly round her shoulders, saying, "Oh, poor Emma. How shocking! How truly dreadful! Just have a good cry."

"I've – I've been crying for the l-last two days," Emma sobbed.

"Of course you have," Charlie said consolingly. "Was Sam taken ill? Do you want to talk about it?"

As Millie had begun to grumble, Emma scrubbed her cheeks and said she had best feed the twins.

Nick tactfully volunteered to make some hot drinks and handed Joel over to Charlie before heading for the kitchen. Dan was not quite sure what to make of his mother holding someone else's baby, and toddled over to take a look, tugging at his mother's skirt to make sure that she gave him some attention, but when he found that she was perfectly well able to speak to him and admire the toy he was clutching, he soon lost interest in the small encumbrance and headed back to his toy box and his own amusements.

Charlie seemed to be at a loss to know what to say or do next and eventually Emma broke the awkward silence. "I'm so sorry to turn up unannounced on your doorstep," she apologised unsteadily, once Millie had settled down to feed. "I came out for a walk but it started to rain so heavily and I didn't want the twins to get soaked, so I just called in on the off-chance. I'll go as soon as they've been fed."

"Not if it's still raining," Charlie protested warmly. "Stay as long as you like. When I saw you last Sunday, I told you to come round with the twins sometime."

"Yes, but not out of the blue – and not in such - such difficult circumstances! I truly didn't mean to turn up and make a scene. I'm really sorry to land all this on you."

"For goodness sake, don't be silly," Charlie reassured her. "That's what friends are for. We'll do whatever we can to help – you'd do the same for me. Do you want to tell me about Sam?"

Emma shook her head, not in rebuff but in despair. "You know he always cycled to work? He was knocked off his bike in the rush hour on Tuesday morning," she explained, her voice shaking precariously. "They told me he was killed almost instantly – could hardly have known anything about it. He –." Her throat closed and she could say no more.

Charlie patted her shoulder.

"How awful! And such a shock for you! Has anyone been looking after you?"

"The police have been very kind. They kept an eye on me on Tuesday and they sent a - a family liaison officer round yesterday."

"What about your own family? Couldn't one of them come and stay with you for a bit?"

"It's not that easy," Emma explained. "My brother is out in Singapore and my sister has got three children of her own to think about and get to school and all their other activities. She might come down at the weekend, she says, if her husband isn't too busy to keep an eye on them. And Mum and Dad can't fly home just now. It's sometimes problematic for them to get travel documents – plus they were here for a week just after the twins were born and it's too expensive for them to fly home very often."

"But that's dreadful! You need some support at a time like this. What about church?"

"I'm sure people will do what they can, but I haven't

told anyone yet. You're the first – apart from my immediate family – and Nick."

"Yes, I hope you don't mind about running into Nick. If I'd known you were going to call I'd have arranged for him to be elsewhere, but I guess that's all ancient history now anyway – and you've got worse things to think about. When I first got home, I thought for a moment that he'd upset you, but that was just me being silly. So much water has passed under the bridge that I'm sure you two can meet without high drama."

"Don't worry about it," Emma said tonelessly.

"So, when are you planning to let folk at church know what's happened? Do you want me to make some phone calls?"

"To be honest, I don't have a plan. I just haven't been able to think straight to work out what calls I should make – nor what I should say. I sat down to figure it out this morning but it was all too difficult and I just bundled Joel and Millie up and came out for a walk – running away from my problems. But of course I can't do that – so stupid! My brain seems to have stopped working properly."

"It's the shock," Charlie said. "I'm sure it's only natural. Let me go and see how Nick's getting on with making the drinks. You look as though you could really do with one. Come along, Dan," she added. "Let's go through to the kitchen. You'd like some juice, wouldn't you?"

Dan hurried to the door as fast as his sturdy little legs would carry him and Charlie bustled out with her son, still carrying baby Joel over her shoulder.

Left alone, Emma shut her eyes for a moment. She was so tired – beyond exhausted – but as soon as she closed her eyes, distressing images arose in her mind to torment her. She frowned and forced her eyes open again. "Lord," she prayed, as she had done repeatedly in the last two days, "Lord, please help me."

She hadn't once managed to progress any further in prayer, to ask for anything specific or to flesh out the request in any way, but she recognised that she was desperately in need of help. Her circumstances were challenging enough – the sudden loss of her husband, twins who were only eleven weeks old, no income and no idea how she would manage – but worse was the poisonous mixture of disbelief, anger, guilt and regret that had been churning through her mind since the courteous and sympathetic visit from the police, who had broken the news to her on Tuesday morning.

She was horrified to find that she wanted to scream at Sam, to tell him that she'd never liked the way he insisted on cycling to work, that it had been selfish and sanctimonious and dangerous, and that he had been an idiot to take the risk when he had only recently become a father. She wanted him to know that he had left her in an almost impossible situation and that it was all because of his pig-headed determination to keep fit, and to save the environment along with a few paltry pennies. Now she was left to face the future alone and she was terrified.

At the same time, she couldn't truly believe that he was dead. She wondered whether it could all be a mistake, a nightmare, a hoax. On Tuesday and again on Wednesday evening she had imagined that he would call and tell her he was on his way home from work, as he had done every evening since they were married; she heard his footsteps on the path, his key in the lock. This morning she had walked into the bathroom expecting him to be there, shaving. The mind and the memory played cruel tricks.

In fact, at the moment her mind was the enemy. It replayed the events of Tuesday in an unremitting loop, showing her not only the police visit, the shocking words that had destroyed the life she had so carefully built with Sam, the careful revelation of such details of the accident as she needed to know and all that she had subsequently had to endure, but also images she had never seen and never wanted to imagine: Sam on his bike hitting the pothole and swerving into the path of the van, as one eyewitness had reportedly described, his body being dragged under the wheels and being left battered and broken. If she tried to remember how he had looked as he had set off for work that Tuesday morning, she would see superimposed on that memory a horrible picture of his injuries, as she envisaged them in her mind's eye.

And then there were the regrets: "If I'd known we would have less than two years of marriage, I would have been more patient, more loving," she thought. "I would have held my tongue when he forgot to put the bins out or when he pointed out that something needed doing and I was just about to do it anyway; I wouldn't have minded when he didn't always understand that I was joking; I would have tried harder to show more gratitude for all that he did, supporting us and loving us." And so it went on, as she kept thinking of other ways in which she had failed as a wife.

Her thoughts were fixed on the same treadmill for much of the day and night. Only the needs of the twins were capable of catching her attention for long amidst the press of emotions arising from the tragedy.

Emma became aware that Mille had finished feeding. She lifted her up against her shoulder and patted her small, warm back. In the quiet, she could faintly hear Joel complaining in the distance and just as she was wondering wearily whether she should go in search of him, Charlotte came back into the room bearing a mug of steaming tea.

With the door open, Joel's cries could be heard more clearly and Emma got quickly to her feet, instinctively moving to satisfy his demands, but Charlie told her firmly to sit down again and not go anywhere. She put the mug down on a mat on the coffee table rather emphatically and removed Millie from Emma's shoulder, repeating her command to sit down. "You can have your tea before you feed Joel," she said. "You need to look after yourself too. It's more important than ever now – if you get ill or anything, whatever would happen to the twins?"

"Oh, but -," Emma began, but she did sit down again, trying to suppress the fear which rose in her as her imagination pictured an illness that rendered her incapable of caring for the twins.

"No 'buts'!" Charlie replied, seating herself in another armchair with Millie on her lap. "Relax and drink up. Nick is perfectly capable of putting up with Joel for a few more minutes."

"I was thinking of Joel, not Nick," Emma replied defensively, as she took a grateful sip of the wonderful, hot tea.

"Well, don't. It won't do him any harm to wait a little longer. They're tough little things."

Emma cradled the warm mug of tea in her hands and leant back in the armchair, watching her friend play with

Millie and determined to try and think of something other than Sam's death and its consequences.

"What's Nick doing here anyway?" she asked after a moment, hoping she did not sound too accusing.

"He's got a series of meetings in London this week."

"But not today?"

"I think there's some event this evening. He was up in Town all day Tuesday and Wednesday, and I know he's out for most of tomorrow; then I think there's a conference on Saturday, and he'll head back up to York on Sunday."

"Is that where he lives now?"

"Yes."

"I hadn't realised Ed and Nick were still such good friends."

"They're not really. They phone or email occasionally, but they haven't seen each other much lately – not since Nick moved up north to work."

"It's quite friendly to put someone up for a week," Emma pointed out.

"Oh, that came about completely by chance," Charlie replied, happy to have something ordinary to talk about. "Nick had arranged to stay with his aunt who lives six or seven miles away from us, over in Banstead, but when he arrived on Monday evening, there was no one there. It turned out that her daughter had been taken ill and she'd rushed down to Devon earlier in the day to help with the grandchildren. She'd forgotten all about Nick. So there he was stranded on her doorstep at ten o'clock at night, with nowhere to sleep. He phoned Ed to ask whether he knew of any decent hotels in the area but of course, in the circumstances, Ed immediately said he should come and stay here."

Emma had finished her mug of tea by now, so she stated her intention of finding Joel. Charlie, carrying Millie, led the way, although Emma would have had no difficulty tracking Joel down by following the sound of his cries.

When Charlie opened the kitchen door, Nick was discovered pacing out the length of the large kitchen and jigging Joel gently up and down, while talking softly to him.

Emma could not hear what was being said over the baby's protests but she felt unaccountably resentful at the sight of Nick holding Joel.

"Thank you for looking after him," she said stiffly and went speedily to reclaim her child, heading straight back to the sitting room, where Joel could have his turn in peace.

CHAPTER 2

Charlotte insisted that her friend should stay for lunch and, when they had each put a clean nappy on a twin and washed their hands in Charlie's smart, spotless bathroom, Emma was ushered back into the spacious and smartly furbished kitchen, to find that an attractive meal of salad, quiche, cheeses and crusty bread had been laid out on the table. Dan was already in his highchair and Charlie brought down his old baby gym and set it up over a mat on the floor.

Nick led them in a short grace, quoted one of the Psalms – '*The Lord is close to the broken-hearted*' – and prayed for Emma, Millie and Joel in one brief sentence, to which Charlie added an emphatic 'Amen'. The twins, docile now they had been changed and were no longer hungry, lay contentedly side by side under the gym throughout lunch, and Emma was able to eat her food in peace, although she had little appetite. Charlie kept one eye on Dan and plied him with suitable sustenance but also chatted to Nick about his plans, while occasionally exhorting Emma to have something more to eat.

Listening with half an ear as she wrestled with the unrestful cycle of her own intractable thoughts, Emma gathered that Nick had been invited down to the head office of his company to undergo a series of interviews, tests and meetings, to ascertain whether he would be a suitable candidate for a vacant post that had arisen there. Nick seemed ambivalent about the opportunity he had been offered. It would plainly be a significant promotion but he explained that he had not intended to move to London.

"Besides," he added, with a brief glance at Emma, who seemed to have withdrawn into herself and was crumbling a piece of bread unseeingly on to her plate, "I always planned to see if I might be accepted for the church at some point, once I'd got a few years of secular work under my belt."

"Train as a minister you mean?"

Nick assented.

"Would taking this new job make that more difficult?" Charlie asked.

"Only that I'd feel a bit awkward accepting a new, more senior post, knowing I'm probably not intending to stay at the company above a year or two."

"I suppose you couldn't tell them? I guess it'd be shooting yourself in the foot."

"As a matter of fact, I've mentioned it a couple of times to my boss in York and I did raise it here on Tuesday morning. I thought they might send me straight home again, but they didn't seem very interested. I'm not sure they believe me."

Emma, who was not as unaware of the conversation as she appeared, found herself remembering that, six years ago, Nick had expressed the same intention of training for ministry one day. He had not changed his mind in that regard, it seemed, whatever other sentiments had altered so radically – always assuming you could rely on anything he said, which was questionable, in her opinion.

It was so important to be able to trust a person, she

mused. Sam had been so very dependable. It would have been anathema to him ever to mislead anyone. His meticulous concern to be entirely clear and unambiguous at all times might sometimes have led him into lengthy explanations and reiterations, but that was surely better than misleading people and letting them down. She had not valued Sam as she should – and now it was too late!

Just as she reached this conclusion, a small internal voice whispered that Sam had let her down more severely than anyone. *He* was the one who, by his own choices, had abandoned her with two small babies. Her involuntary gasp of dismay at this stray thought drew the attention of her companions but they did not press her for an explanation. Instead, they focussed on practicalities and decided that everyone had finished with the first course. Very soon, it had been cleared away and a choice of fruit and yoghurts added to the table.

Emma choose a pear and began to quarter it listlessly.

"Now, I've been thinking." Charlie addressed her friend briskly. "It seems to me that, for all sorts of reasons, you should start letting people know what's happened. You're going to need some support – and I know that people at church will want to help."

"I don't like to – to cause trouble."

"Look at it the other way," Charlie suggested. "If someone else in our church family was struggling, wouldn't you want to know about it so you could help - and at least pray about it?"

"I suppose," Emma conceded reluctantly.

"What do *you* think?" Charlie asked Nick.

"It's Emma's decision, but prayer is always good - and

practical help must be beneficial with two small babies to care for."

"So once you've eaten that pear, shall we call Michael?" Charlie asked Emma. "He's our vicar," she explained to Nick.

Panic rose in Emma at the thought of having to go through the whole account of Sam's death again and having to deal with yet another person's shock and sympathy, but she supposed it would not get any easier and there was no other reason to delay so she nodded mutely.

"Good girl," Charlie said and, correctly interpreting her friend's expression, assured Emma that she would sit with her while she made the call, or even ring the vicar herself, if Emma preferred.

Once lunch was finished, Nick volunteered for washing-up duty while Charlie went to put Dan down in his cot for a nap. Emma picked up a tea towel but Nick told her kindly to sit and rest.

"I don't want to rest!" Emma snapped.

After an uncomfortable pause, she added more civilly but very drearily, "I'm sorry, but I can't rest. It's easier when there's something to do. Otherwise, I think too much – and my thoughts are unbearable at the moment."

Nick frowned down at the washing up bowl but raised no further objection and, between them, they made rapid progress through the collection of dirty plates and cutlery. Charlie rejoined them just as they were finishing and asked Nick whether he could keep an eye on the twins while she and Emma contacted the vicar.

He readily agreed, so Charlie collected the two phone

handsets and she and Emma headed for the sitting room, leaving Nick and the twins in the kitchen.

With Charlie seated beside her on the sofa for moral support and able to listen in on the second handset, Emma hoped she would be brave enough to speak, but her fingers trembled as she dialled the church number and when Margaret, Michael's energetically efficient secretary answered the phone, she could not think of a word to say.

"Ask to speak to Michael," Charlie whispered.

"Oh, yes – er – this is Emma – um – Barton. Could I speak to Michael, please?"

"Can I ask what it's in connection with?"

"Just say it's a personal matter," Charlie advised softly, her hand over the receiver.

"I – er – it's a personal matter," Emma repeated obediently.

"I'll try his line for you," Margaret said competently.

Within seconds, Michael's mild voice could be heard saying, "Good afternoon, Emma. How can I help?"

Emma drew a long breath.

"Sam – my husband – was killed in a road accident on Tuesday," she blurted out, and then stopped. She was on the verge of tears once more and had no idea what else to say.

There was a brief silence but then Michael said compassionately, "I'm very sorry. What a dreadful shock for you. Who is looking after you?"

"I'm with Charlotte Lloyd."

"Good. Now, it will be best if I come round and see you, rather than discussing things over the phone. I'll bring Janet. Will you be at home later this afternoon – at about four?"

"Y-yes," Emma replied uncertainly, realising from his wise and professional reaction that he had probably had to deal with many testing conversations over his years as a vicar.

"Then we'll see you at four," he concluded. "Goodbye."

Charlie's immediate concern was to ascertain whether her friend wanted support at the four o'clock meeting.

"He's bringing his wife," Emma pointed out, thinking that she had imposed on Charlie enough for one day. "I'll be okay. Janet's very kind."

"And she does a lot of the pastoral care," Charlie agreed. She looked at her watch and added, "I guess you'd better be going soon, if they're turning up at your house at four. I wish I could offer you a lift but we don't have two baby car seats. I suppose your pushchair isn't one of those convertible types?"

"No, but it's stopped raining," Emma pointed out, nodding towards the view of the sunny street that could be seen from the window.

As they walked back to the kitchen together, Charlie gave her friend a little lecture about the importance of looking after herself and accepting any help that was offered. "Twins are a huge amount of work," she stated unnecessarily. "Frankly, *one* baby was pretty exhausting!"

In the kitchen, they found Nick sitting cross-legged on the floor next to Joel, shaking a toy for him to watch, while holding Millie on his lap. "I think they're getting a bit bored," he said. "Or tired, perhaps?"

"I'll take them home," Emma said, finding it peculiarly irritating to see him looking so much at home with the twins.

She began to gather her things together and went to

fetch the babies' outdoor clothes. Kneeling down beside Joel, she set to work to ease his little limbs into his snowsuit. Unsolicited, Nick knelt beside her and began to dress Millie, while Charlie continued to proffer advice and encouragement.

"You must try and give yourself a break now and then, if you can," she said. "Talk it through with Janet and see what kind of help might be available. If you want, you can come and stay here for a bit – if you'd like some company. And you know you can always call me if – when! – there's anything I can do – or Ed, of course."

Emma thanked her friend warmly but she could not bring herself to thank Nick and, as soon as Joel was wrapped up and ready to go in the pushchair, she told him that she could manage Millie herself. He stood up without comment and retreated a few steps but continued to irritate her by watching her as she finished the task.

At Emma's request, Charlie helped her carry the twins to the pushchair and soon they were strapped in and ready to go. Emma shrugged herself into her damp coat and said goodbye to her friend.

"I'll call you," Charlie said, kissing her on both cheeks and then clasping her in an affectionate embrace.

"Thank you," Emma replied, close to tears again. "Thanks for everything. You've been so kind."

"Nonsense!" Charlie returned, bracingly. "Now off you go. We'll speak later."

Emma looked doubtfully at Nick who had propped one shoulder against the doorframe between the kitchen and the hall.

"Take care of yourself," he said with some reserve.

"Goodbye," she replied formally and turned to go, but found him beside her a moment later, lifting the pushchair out over the front doorstep.

"Thank you," she muttered stiffly and headed away down the path, only to have him follow and open the garden gate for her to manoeuvre the pushchair through more easily.

She raised a hand to Charlie and walked away self-consciously but without a backward glance. She was glad to turn the corner at the end of the street and know that she was out of sight.

The weather had reverted to bright April breeziness and she put her head down into the wind and walked briskly towards home. Although her thoughts were no brighter than before, she felt that she had benefitted a little from Charlie's company and support. The time at her friend's house had provided a little respite in the otherwise unremitting fog of distress and boundless struggle which seemed to face her at every turn.

It was unfortunate that Nick Knight had been there and even more unfortunate that he had not had the decency to take himself off and mind his own business, she thought savagely, suppressing the small voice in her mind which pointed out that he had actually been quite useful. "I didn't *want* him to be useful," she argued with herself. "He's done more than enough damage in the past. I never wanted to see him again and now here he is, interfering without so much as a 'by your leave'. He must have known that the whole situation was desperately uncomfortable. Mind you, he plainly has no conscience or he would never have treated me so badly six years ago. He just hasn't changed at all." With this conclusion, she dismissed him from her conscious thoughts and tried with little success to plan for the meeting with Michael and Janet. Her mind would only rest on the topic for a few seconds and would then lead her off at a tangent into regret or anxiety.

Millie and Joel fell asleep on the way home and, when Emma arrived back at the compact, modern, detached house Sam had bought for them, she was able to lift the pushchair carefully into the house and wheel it through to the sitting room, leaving them to their slumbers. They were still asleep when the vicar and his wife arrived, and Emma invited the visitors through to her kitchen where they sat at the dining table, so that the first and most difficult part of the meeting was accomplished without any more distractions than Emma keeping alert in case the twins should wake and, of course, the oppression of her own troubled thoughts.

Michael and Janet made an extremely effective and thorough team. They offered genuine sympathy and sincere concern and, once they were acquainted with a few more of the facts, they made it a priority to open the Bible and to pray for Emma, Millie and Joel in thoughtful detail. Michael concluded by reading Psalm One Hundred and Thirty: "Out of the depths I cry to you O Lord; O Lord, hear my voice… I wait for the Lord, my soul waits, and in his word I put my hope… for with the Lord is unfailing love and with him is full redemption."

Their enquiries were sensitively made and they did not attempt to offer impossible or unwelcome comfort when Emma lost her composure, but they helped her to begin to think through the arrangements which would eventually have to be made once Sam's body was released. They asked gently about the ownership of the house, plainly concerned that she might have to leave if she could not meet rent or mortgage costs, and were delighted to learn that Sam had bought the property outright with a legacy from his parents, and had also been able to put some of his inheritance into savings, which Emma hoped would make the future easier. Michael mentioned that he knew of a solicitor in the congregation who would be able to help in matters of probate, if there were complications.

Although understanding the cause, they were plainly troubled by the lack of familial support available for Emma and were not greatly reassured by the faint prospect of a visit from Emma's older sister, Rachel, at the weekend. Janet questioned her rather closely about Rachel's situation and asked why, if her husband was often busy at weekends, she could not find someone else to keep an eye on her children in the exceptional and tragic circumstances. "Doesn't she have friends or in-laws? I can't believe there's no-one who could help."

"I don't know," Emma replied helplessly. "I think her in-laws are nearby but maybe they're busy too."

"Then, if she can't leave her children, why doesn't she invite you to go up and stay with *her*?"

"They don't really have space. They've got a four-bedroomed house and three children."

"That's ridiculous!" Janet exclaimed, although Michael shook his head at her in slight reproof. "I'm sorry to criticise your sister," she went on a little more temperately, "but I can't believe that a couple of the children couldn't share a room for a little while, so as to accommodate you."

"I should think they would hate it," Emma replied candidly. "Besides, Harry – Rachel's husband – works long hours at a very high-powered job and needs his sleep, so two babies who are liable to cry in the night would hardly be ideal guests."

"These all sound like excuses to me – and very selfish ones, at that!"

"Maybe, but it hardly makes me inclined to push for an invitation. Anyway, I'm not really that keen to go. All our things are here and everything is familiar, and – my sister and I don't – well, we're very different."

"Come and stay with us," Janet offered impulsively. "We've got two spare bedrooms now Freddie and Archie have left home, and we won't be at all bothered by a little bit of noise in the night."

"You're very kind. Thank you *so* much," Emma said, very grateful for such thoughtfulness and mindful of the great contrast with her sister's lukewarm concern. "But I – I think I'd rather stay here, if you don't mind." She could not imagine uprooting herself and the twins from their own home, however empty and strange it now felt, and she could not begin to think about what she would need to pack if they were to leave.

"Of course, dear. Whatever you prefer," Janet replied warmly. "I just don't like the idea of you on your own – especially at night. Would it help if I stayed here for a night or two? Perhaps till your sister turns up at the weekend – if she turns up!"

"Don't forget you're speaking at a meeting on Saturday morning," Michael reminded his wife.

"I haven't forgotten, but I can always find a substitute. *Someone* needs to put Emma first in this dreadful situation!"

"It's alright," Emma interposed gently. "I think I can

manage. I've already managed for two nights. But it's *so* kind of you to offer – and perhaps I can let you know if I change my mind or if I need help sometime? To be honest, one of the things that's really worrying me is how I'll cope if I'm ever ill and there's no-one to look after the twins."

"Just call us at any time," Michael said kindly.

His wife agreed and proposed that they think through the provision of meals by the pastoral care team as well as baby-sitting and any other help Emma thought she might need. "I'd suggest that you allow me to organise a rota to cover all the evening meals for the next week or two, at least. That way you can be sure of one decent hot meal a day, without having to worry about finding time to prepare it, with all that you'll be dealing with at the moment."

"That would be really kind. In some ways, it's not so much finding the time as that I can't really be bothered to think about what to eat. It all seems to be too much effort just now. It's very different when you're cooking for someone else." She wiped away a tear. "I do know that I've got to look after myself for the sake of the twins," she added. "Charlie was reminding me earlier - but I *had* already thought of it, and I will try to be sensible."

"You're doing amazingly well," Janet told her sincerely. "And you're so rational. I'm full of admiration."

Emma did not feel rational. She felt as though every thought and word was filtered through a confused haze of anger, doubt and despair. She was about to confess as much when their conversation was interrupted by a faint cry from the sitting room. Further complaint followed and Emma excused herself and went to lift Joel out of the pushchair. Glancing at the clock, she realised that both twins would soon be hungry and guessed that Millie would wake before long. She said as much to her visitors when she carried Joel back to the kitchen.

Michael rose to his feet at once and suggested to his wife that they leave Emma in peace.

"Very shortly," Janet agreed, and turned back to Emma. "Now, just to summarise: Michael will be in touch again in a few days to discuss the format of the service a bit more; I'll go away and sort out a rota for evening meals for the next fortnight; and we've agreed that you'll ring us if there's any other help you need or even if you just want company or someone to talk to. In the meantime, what are you planning to eat for supper this evening?"

"I don't know. I haven't thought."

"In that case," Janet said energetically, "I'll pop back in a couple of hours with some fish pie. That's what *we're* having for tea - and there'll be plenty to spare."

Emma thanked them both for their many kindnesses and, with Joel over her shoulder, escorted them to the front door. As she waved goodbye, she could hear Millie beginning to stir, and by the time she had fed Joel, his sister was in full cry. Once Millie was satisfied, they needed changing, and then Emma realised that, if she did not sort the washing and run at least one load, they would soon have nothing clean to wear. She laid the twins down in their cots for safety and went to rectify matters.

CHAPTER 3

Emptying the linen basket was an enormous mistake, for at the bottom, under the jumble of her own clothes, tumbled with babygros and blankets, were the clothes that Sam had worn to work on Monday and had shed at the end of a busy day. She sat on the floor by the basket and wept bitterly, head in hands. At some level, she was aware of how ridiculous she must look, sitting crying beside a pile of dirty washing; but there was no-one to see or care, so what did it matter?

That was the worst of it, she decided: there was *no-one* anymore. Sam would have cared. He had thought the world of his wife and had wanted to shield her from every difficulty. He had always been a doting husband who could see no fault in her, and when the twins had arrived he had become almost worshipful of her from joy in his offspring and gratitude for the gift of fatherhood. She recalled how he had held the twins so proudly when they were first born, one in the crook of each arm, and had praised her superlatively for their safe arrival and for their perfection.

In the eleven short weeks since then – weeks filled with feeding and changing, sleepless nights of pacing the floor and rocking prams, anxieties over rate of growth and ability to smile – Sam had been completely committed to playing his part as a parent, whenever he was at home. He had taken his turn at all the tasks that could be shared and had repeatedly told Emma what a wonderful wife and mother she was.

All that was gone – finished when he had hit that pothole and ended his life so needlessly under that van. "Why, Lord? Why?" Emma asked, and the question re-echoed around her mind as if it could not escape to reach the God she had known and spoken to all her life.

She wondered, not for the first time, what had gone through Sam's mind as he had sped inexorably towards the van. Had he known it was the end of his life on earth? Had he prayed? Had he thought of her – of the twins? Had he seen the bitter irony in the manner of his passing? He had been the most law-abiding, careful cyclist you could imagine. He had prided himself on never having had an accident. He wore all the right high-visibility and protective gear, he maintained his bike in perfect condition, he strictly obeyed the rules of the road, and yet no-one could fully protect themselves from such random hazards. If anything, he had exposed himself to additional hazards by his inexplicable insistence on cycling so much.

No, that was wrong, Emma reminded herself fiercely. He could have had a random accident anywhere – crossing a road as a pedestrian, in a car, under a train. It was useless to apportion blame – worse than useless, since it tarnished her memories of Sam. The only blame was her own for not making more of the short time they had had together.

Hearing the beginning of grumblings from the twins, Emma made an effort to pull herself together, drying her eyes and wiping her nose; but her eyes felt so swollen that she went to the bathroom and bathed them quickly in cold water, patting them dry and hastening back to collect Millie and Joel.

Both were inclined to be a little fractious, as was often the case in the early evening, and Emma was fully occupied in endeavouring to entertain and soothe one and then the other, while watching the clock wearily round to bath-time. If Janet had not returned as promised with a portion of fish pie, Emma might well have managed only toast for her evening meal, as she had done on the previous two evenings.

Taking stock of the situation, Janet announced that she could stay for a little while. She bustled around, laying the table and serving up the pie, while Emma buckled Millie and Joel into their two bouncy chairs. Then she persuaded Emma to the table and took her place between the twins, showing them musical toys and fabric books and speaking nonsense to them, so that Emma could eat in comparative peace.

Emma forced herself to clear her plate, although it took a great deal of willpower. She was very grateful for the help, the company and the concern, but the painful spiral of her thoughts could not be halted for long and the struggle to maintain any semblance of normality became slowly more difficult as exhaustion set in. In some ways it was a relief when Janet took her leave and Emma could admit defeat and surrender to her misery once more.

She bathed Millie and Joel in turn, washing them gently, drying and dressing them with extra care and lingering over the process because their warmth and solid reality seemed a lifeline in a world of chaos, their total helplessness was a reason for Emma to keep going, and their unconsciousness of their loss made it almost possible to pretend for a little while that nothing had changed; although she knew that *everything* had changed, that nothing would ever be the same again.

Once the twins were in their cots and had settled to sleep, Emma went wearily downstairs to clear up and lock up for the night. The house felt strangely empty and alien but Emma chided herself for an overactive imagination and went to work methodically to tidy each room, as Sam would have liked.

In the middle of this process the phone rang. The ringing seemed unduly loud in the quiet house; Emma was torn between dread of a trying conversation and fear that the noise might disturb the twins. Heart thumping ridiculously, she snatched the handset up and hesitantly identified herself.

"It's okay. It's only me – Charlie," came her friend's voice. "I said I'd call."

"Oh, yes. Thank you." Emma was greatly relieved to find that she would not be faced with more explanations and commiserations.

"How did you get on with Michael and Janet?" Charlie asked.

"They were very kind and helpful. Janet's going to organise a rota to provide evening meals for a couple of weeks, and I can ask for other help if I need it."

"Is there anything I can do?"

"I – I can't think of anything right now."

"Well, that's understandable; but at some point you'll probably find there are things you'd be glad of a hand with. So just let me know when they come to mind. Okay? Promise me! No thinking that you don't like to trouble me or I'll be really cross."

"Okay. *Thank* you."

Charlie brushed aside Emma's gratitude, told her that she would drop round sometime the following day and rang off. It had only been a short call but Emma appreciated it enormously. It showed a genuine thoughtfulness and concern and a willingness to act, which eased Emma's burden a little. Between Charlie's call and Michael and Janet's support, Emma was able to retire to bed at the end of the evening feeling that a tiny glimmer of light had pierced the darkness which pressed in on her.

Sleep was still elusive and her thoughts were still mainly focussed on her anger over the tragedy, her regrets for the past, her desperate loneliness in the present and her fears for the future, but she found herself able to pray, to pour out to God all her emotions and anxieties and, although she felt no less stressed or fearful, she did at least feel that she had been heard.

The twins woke in the small hours as usual, requiring feeding, and were slow to settle. Of intent, Emma turned her thoughts to the day just passed and thanked God for the promised support of her church family, for Michael and Janet's kindness and for Charlie's longstanding friendship. How odd it was to have seen Nick again after all these years, she reflected, and on such a day. He hadn't changed much to look at, she mused, but she supposed he would not be able to say the same for her in her current circumstances. Had she met him in the normal run of things, she would have been inclined to have nothing to do with him after the way he had behaved six years ago, but she had not really been given that option. He ought to be thoroughly ashamed of himself. In truth, he had seemed a little ill at ease and perhaps his readiness to assist with the twins had sprung from a guilty conscience. He had tried so hard to be helpful. Not that it made any difference. His past behaviour had been contemptible and there was no reason why anyone should trust him. The old hurt and resentment stirred briefly, but then Emma recalled that she had far bigger things to worry about than being let down by an old boyfriend.

Her immediate concerns sprang back into the forefront of her mind. How on earth was she going to cope with bringing up the twins on her own? Both practically and financially, it would be an enormous challenge, let alone spiritually. Before the events of this week, it had never crossed her mind to imagine that there was any real risk that she could find herself in such a situation – and it was terrifying! Every time she thought of it, her heart raced in horror and anger rose up in her: anger towards Sam, who had left her in this dreadful mess, and anger towards God, who had allowed it to happen and who presumably expected her to cope. Only she wasn't coping: she was exhausted and afraid. "You'll have to help me, Lord," she prayed. "There's no way I can do this on my own."

A phrase from John's Gospel came to mind: 'I will not leave you as orphans.' She wondered whether it was a message meant for her or just a coincidence and on that thought she fell asleep.

Millie and Joel were awake again before six o'clock: another day had begun.

Emma's parents rang before she had eaten breakfast. They both worked in a hospital in Nepal and, because of the time difference, were phoning during their lunchbreak. They were plainly concerned for their younger daughter but not disposed to articulate their concern in words of sympathy. The needs of the poor and disadvantaged patients they saw daily were so very great that Emma could not avoid the suspicion that they rather thought all Westerners over-indulged and unduly feeble. Certainly, they confined their conversation to sound practical advice and to a promise that one of them would endeavour to return to England for the funeral, once a date had been settled. It seemed that their strong sense of duty to the people in their care made it impossible for both of them to abandon their posts at short notice, but they had discussed the situation and agreed that it would be right for one of them to support Emma at such a time.

"So do let us know the date as soon as you can," her mother urged her.

"Yes, I will," Emma promised.

"And try to arrange things expeditiously," her father directed. "There's no point in delay."

"I don't think I can do anything until I hear from the coroner – or whoever deals with this kind of thing."

"You can put everything else in place so that things can go ahead as soon as you do hear," he pointed out.

"I spoke to our vicar about it yesterday," Emma assured him, "and he'll be in touch about the details of the service in a few days – after the weekend, I guess."

"Chase him up if you don't hear anything in the early part of next week" her father told her firmly. "Here, we always have to chase everything several times before there's any progress."

Emma did not think Michael would need pursuing but she did not say so. The call concluded with admonitions from her mother to eat sensibly and to rest when the twins were sleeping, and Emma responded suitably but found herself slightly resentful of the way they were able to reduce every situation to simple practicalities, as if one were a fool ever to find things difficult.

Later that morning, her brother, Luke, called from Singapore.

"Hello, Sis."

"Oh, Luke! Thanks for ringing."

"No worries. Heard the news from Mum and Dad yesterday. So sorry about Sam – nice chap. How are you coping?"

"As you might imagine really: not very well."

"It's early days – and you've got your hands full with the twins. I was reading Two Corinthians Four this morning and I thought of you. Have a look sometime."

"Thanks. I will."

"When's the funeral?"

"Nothing's been decided yet but I'll let you know as soon as I hear."

"Cheers. I'll make sure I'm there. I have to be over in the UK on business at some point soon, so I'm hoping to combine the two visits. That way, I get to fly at the firm's expense – business class – always nice. I was planning to drop in anyway – I want to meet my new niece and nephew."

"That'd be good. Mum or Dad will probably come over too. They weren't sure which one of them it would be and they didn't think they could both come, but one of them will try and make it."

"So they said when they called me. First, they said they were bothered about the cost of flights so I told them I'd pay if that helped; but then they decided they still couldn't both go home at short notice so soon after their last visit. They're a funny pair!"

"Are *you* paying for one of them to come?"

"Yeah, but it's no problem. You should have your parents with you at a time like this."

"It's very kind of you."

"Like I said, I'll probably get my flights for free, so it's no big deal. Now, are you okay financially, do you know? How have things been left?"

"I've got no idea yet, but I know I need to find out."

"When you do, let me know if there's anything I can do to assist. I've got way more than I can ever spend, so just shout."

"Thanks. *Thank you*, Luke. I really appreciate the offer."

"Well, you're not going to get anything from Rachel – she spends every penny on her little darlings. And Mum and Dad aren't in a position to help."

"They give plenty of advice," Emma said, sounding tarter than she intended.

Her brother snorted. "Let me guess! Eat healthily, get to bed early, brush your teeth and make sure you've got a clean hanky! Statements of the obvious. Ignore it – I do! Anyway, I've got to go; I'm off to a client dinner. I'll be praying. Phone me when there's an update. God bless."

Emma was used to his abrupt manner and blunt statements and was grateful for his interest. He made contact very rarely but she recognised from his offers of help that he had a genuine concern for her welfare.

She was not sure she could say the same for her sister,

Rachel, who rang during the afternoon to explain volubly why she would be unable to visit the following day.

"Harry is frantically busy with work just now. I asked him if he could look after the children but he says it's utterly impossible. He's frightfully sorry because he knows you must be having an awful time, but he's got a couple of clients who are ridiculously demanding. You wouldn't believe the time and energy it takes humouring them. It wouldn't be so bad if he could just sit in the study and deal with phone calls and emails, but Tilly has horse riding and Jago has started playing rugby and Clemmie has been invited to a party. As it is, I'm going to have to spend the whole of Saturday afternoon ferrying them around. I'm just an unpaid taxi service. You wait till yours get to this stage and you'll see what I mean. I'm run off my feet."

Emma did not feel inclined to sympathise, and neither did Charlie when she called by a little later. In fact, she roundly condemned Rachel's self-absorption and rigid adherence to routine. "I'll bet she could have found someone else to give the children lifts, but it's easier for her to run them about than to give it any thought or to ask other mums for a favour. She's too much in love with her safe, middleclass lifestyle; she probably adores being seen at all these socially acceptable places dropping off her privileged kids in her four-wheel drive and complaining about being the family chauffeur. Oh well, at least we know it's no good relying on her for anything!"

"How d'you know she's got a four-wheel drive?" Emma asked. She was sitting with one of the twins on her lap, while rocking the other in a car seat with her foot.

"Inevitable! Now, I've brought round a chicken

casserole," Charlie went on, delving in her bag and lifting out a lidded storage container. "I reckon there's a couple of portions there, so you could freeze half or have it tomorrow as well. There are potatoes already in it, so it's a complete meal. Just heat it up again. I had a word with Janet earlier and she's planning to start the rota on Monday but she told me to let you know that she'll drop round with a plated roast dinner on Sunday. What can I do to help now I'm here?"

"Where's Dan?"

"Nick's keeping an eye on him. He got back from London about half an hour ago and when he realised we were coming over, he suggested that I might be more help to you if I didn't have Dan with me – which is quite right, but I didn't like to ask. So now you have to make use of me. Would you like me to take the twins? What can I do?"

"Perhaps you could help me work out who else I should be notifying. I started a list, but I didn't get very far."

"Sure. Where's the list?"

Once they'd located it, the two of them sat and thought through which people and organisations would need to know of Sam's death. Between them, they jotted down banks, building societies, insurers, various service and utility providers, government bodies, organisations to which Sam had paid subscriptions, friends and so on. Charlie looked up as many of the contact details as she could find online and added them to the list.

"Presumably, his employer knows?" Charlie asked tentatively.

"Yes. The police dealt with that on Tuesday. Although, I suppose I ought to let them know about the funeral arrangements - once it's organised."

"What about Sam's family? Have they all been told?"

"He didn't have much in the way of family. Both his parents died a while ago – his dad died when Sam was about ten – not a long-lived family! There are a couple of great aunts and a cousin. I don't think he kept in touch with anyone else."

"Not a very abundant family either, by the sound of it," Charlie remarked, adding Sam's relatives to the list. "Do you want to start contacting some of these people?"

"Not now. I've had enough for one day – and you should go home to Dan. He'll be wanting his tea soon – and so will Joel and Millie – but thank you so much for your help."

CHAPTER 4

When Emma found a moment to look at the Bible verses her brother had mentioned, she found great encouragement in Paul's familiar words: in the reminder that God said 'Let light shine out of darkness', the promise that 'the one who raised the Lord Jesus from the dead will also raise us with Jesus' and the exhortation to fix her eyes 'not on what is seen, but on what is unseen'. In her own deep valley of darkest shadow, she clung on to the knowledge that there was hope of eternal glory.

From Monday, the rota swung into action and over the ensuing days, evening meals began to appear. They were delivered in a variety of different formats, at a wide range of times and in differing ways. Some of the offerings were handed over awkwardly, as if the donor were embarrassed either by their own generosity or by Emma's situation. Emma felt certain that some of the ladies were reluctant to engage in conversation for fear of being obliged to refer to her loss or to deal with any disconcerting displays of emotion, while others seemed uncomfortable with the role of visible philanthropy or the prospect of having to accept her gratitude.

By contrast, some meals were delivered with more of a flourish: a declaration of sympathy and details of the recipe, proffered together with enthusiastic generosity. Some of these ladies wanted to coo over the twins and volunteer to babysit, while others offered practical help with housework or shopping.

In the early days, Emma accepted a number of these pressing offers of help, partly because she was aware that she was not coping very well by herself but largely because she lacked the energy to resist. Besides, the twins took up so much of her time and she was very much aware that there were still a great many matters arising from Sam's death which needed sorting out so she supposed that she should take advantage of any assistance that was offered, in order to free her up to tackle some of these tasks. However, she found that, even when she was free of encumbrances or distractions, she was often unable to focus on the task she had set herself for long.

She did better on the occasions when Charlie dropped round and helped to keep her going. She could not quite understand why it should be the case when, in the past, she had always concentrated best when left alone; but now, by herself, she would soon become despondent, overwhelmed by the size of a task or the painful memories it evoked, whereas Charlie seemed always undaunted and her cheerful chatter often helped to divert her thoughts at least for a little while from gloomy fears and regrets.

Charlie scattered encouragements and praise throughout her discourse, and Emma was able to glean gems of reassurance amidst inconsequential and light-hearted morsels of information about home and family.

On one occasion, Charlie mentioned in passing that Nick had been offered the job in London. During a subsequent visit, she commented that, since he had reiterated his eventual intention to leave secular employment and go to theological college and his employers had still pressed him to accept the transfer, he had apparently decided to make the move down from York and see what transpired.

Charlie announced this just as she was helping Emma to sort through Sam's wardrobe, so it was not to be expected that Emma would have much attention to spare for anything other than her own tragedy. It did occur to her to wonder briefly whether Nick might see more of Ed once he was based in London, although she was certain that the Capital was large enough for her to be able to avoid crossing his path again any time soon, but the thought was soon dismissed as she coped with the heart-wrenching business of deciding which of Sam's belongings should be taken to charity shops and which should be recycled or disposed of.

Every so often, she was obliged to pause and gather her courage but Charlie did not seem to mind the delay. Emma suspected that her friend must have anticipated it would be a time-consuming task, since she had asked Janet to find a babysitter for the twins and had arranged to come over on a Saturday, so that Ed could take care of Dan for the duration. When Emma apologised for vacillating over any item, Charlie repeatedly replied with reassurances and praise.

"Looking through his effects makes *me* feel shaky and a bit tearful," Charlie confessed at one point, "so I can't imagine what it must be like for *you*. Take all the time you need; and if you want to stop, just say so. We can always do some more another day. You've been amazing."

With this encouragement, Emma pressed on and by

the end of the afternoon there were lots of bags set aside for removal. She gratefully accepted Charlie's offer to deal with them and, having helped her friend to load everything into her car and waved her off, went back inside to seek out the twins, feeling that she had made real headway.

Emma was a little surprised to find that all was quiet indoors. Now she had looked at the time, she expected the twins to be grumbling, as it was a longer than usual stretch since their last feed, and she rehearsed the apology she would have to make to Theresa, the stout lady who had been babysitting for her. However, when she went through to the kitchen, she found that the room was empty. She had not had time to feel more than some slight puzzlement before she spied Theresa's steel grey head of hair through the back window, and realised that she was pushing the double buggy round the garden. Emma rushed to the door, eager to deliver her apology and grant this helpful lady her freedom.

As she hurried forwards remorsefully, she recalled that she had made it very plain to Theresa when she had arrived that, if the twins were unsettled, she should come and find Emma at any time, so she hoped that the twins had only just started to get fractious and that, hearing the sounds of Charlie's departure, Theresa had decided that they must be nearly through with their work and had thought to buy a little more time by wheeling Millie and Joel round the back garden.

"I'm so sorry," Emma called. "I hope they haven't been difficult. You should have come and got me."

"It's no problem," Theresa replied calmly. "I've just got them off to sleep, so if you don't disturb them, you can have a bit more time to yourself."

"That's very kind, but I don't suppose they'll sleep for long - they'll be hungry. Anyway, thank you so much for your help this afternoon. Charlie and I made great progress."

"That's good. I don't think the babies will be hungry for a while, dear," Theresa added complacently. "I gave them a cup of baby milk and a rusk each to suck on."

Emma was speechless with disbelief and horror. The twins had not yet been weaned and Emma had made that perfectly clear, so how could this woman have imagined she was being helpful?

"I thought it would be better to allow you and Charlie to get on without interruption," Theresa went on, in the serene assumption of rectitude.

"But I *told* you to come and find me if they were unsettled!" Emma was close to tears.

"That's alright. I've had children of my own. I'm used to dealing with babies."

"That's not the point. What milk did you give them?" Emma demanded angrily.

"I used one of the cartons you had in the cupboard – although it took me a while to find it. I couldn't work out where you keep your bottles or your sterilising kit, but they both seemed happy to take some from a cup and spoon. I rinsed everything out with boiled water first so there's no need to worry about hygiene."

Emma recalled that a few weeks ago she had bought a couple of cartons of UHT baby milk when they were on special offer and put them away at the back of the cupboard for use at some unspecified future date. She could not believe that a visitor would have taken it upon themselves to poke around in her cupboards to track them down or could have thought it acceptable to make decisions about whether to feed *her* babies or how to sterilise the equipment without any reference to her as the mother, let alone giving them rusks when they had never had solid food before.

"There isn't a steriliser," Emma snapped. "I haven't needed to set it up yet, since I'm feeding the twins myself. Where did you get rusks anyway?" she added angrily. "I know I haven't got any of those tucked away for you to hunt out."

"I always carry a few when I babysit," Theresa replied, oblivious to Emma's sharpness and blithely unaware of any crime. "You should get some. You'll find they're very useful. My children loved them."

"But the twins aren't even on solids yet," Emma objected heatedly.

"Then it's about time they were. Look how soundly they're sleeping."

"I was advised to wait till they're about six months old."

"The experts always have to come up with some new theory, but mine were weaned long before then and it hasn't done them any harm. There's no need to get yourself in a state, dear. Of course you'll be emotional at the moment because you've just lost your husband. I know exactly how you're feeling. My husband died five years ago, but he'd been ill for years. Now, I've left your supper in a box in the fridge, so let's lift the pushchair indoors and then I'll be on my way. Make the most of the peace and quiet. I'm pleased to know I haven't lost my touch," she finished, sounding to Emma unbearably smug.

Emma was very tempted to give this opinionated woman a piece of her mind but several considerations halted her. Firstly, she was so angry that, if she began to voice the resentment seething within her, she might say something unforgiveable. Secondly, Theresa had generously agreed to join the rota, had given up her time to be there and had brought Emma some supper as well; and thirdly, Emma did not want to cause any unpleasantness which might be relayed to Janet and upset her, after all her kindness. As a result, she held her tongue but, as soon as she had seen Theresa off the premises, she burst into angry tears and stormed back into the kitchen, slamming the door furiously, almost willing it to wake the twins so that she need not be beholden to anyone so crassly interfering.

While the twins slept on, oblivious to their mother's distress, Emma raged inwardly and impotently, silently rehearsing all the things she would have liked to say to Theresa, but after a few minutes she pulled herself together and made herself a cup of tea – that panacea for all ills.

As she sat at the kitchen table and drank it, she tried to assess a little more calmly why she was so upset at what had taken place. Aside from Theresa's offensive and arrogant suggestion that she knew exactly what Emma was feeling, she couldn't decide whether she most resented the fact that her role as parent had been usurped when her right to make significant decisions on behalf of her children had been ignored or the fact that, because her instructions had been disregarded, she had been cheated of a milestone in the twins' lives – their first solid food had been administered by someone else. It was also concerning to think that Theresa's actions contravened current professional advice, which recommended weaning at about six months. She was sensible enough to realise that one brief breach of the guidelines was unlikely to cause major damage to her babies, but as a conscientious parent she would still have preferred to avoid any breach. Moreover, as she had no intention of using any more formula milk in the near future, the rest of the opened carton would now have to be wasted.

On that thought, Emma went straight to the fridge to remove the carton and tip the contents defiantly down the sink. In the process, she spied the container of food left by Theresa in the fridge for her supper. Extracting it, she found that the old ice cream carton, which was unappetisingly battered and stained, contained a portion of rather grey-looking mince in gravy. On closer inspection, she saw that there were a number of short hairs adhering to a sticky patch on the lid of the box and, quite revolted, she scraped the unpleasant offering into the bin with perverse satisfaction and resigned herself to toast for tea.

As the twins continued to slumber, Emma began to fear that the change in routine would adversely affect all three of them and contemplated trying to wake them. It would have gone very much against the grain to interrupt their rest and she was glad that, before she had to resort to such extreme measures, Millie awoke of her own accord and her complaints soon roused her brother. However, Emma had been right in suspecting that their sleep pattern would be disrupted by the unscheduled events of the day and her resentment over Theresa's unwarranted interference was increased by an unusually broken night.

Emma could not resist sharing her irritation with Charlie next time they spoke and she was glad to find that her friend was equally indignant and rather more forthright. They both agreed, however, that it would be best to say nothing, as it was unlikely that Emma would be obliged to endure Theresa's services very frequently and they could think of no tactful way of reporting her transgressions. It was therefore rather disconcerting to have Janet call a few days later to enquire as to Emma's wellbeing. Apparently, Theresa had felt it necessary to inform Janet that, in her opinion, Emma was highly emotional and irrational. "She seemed to think you had been upset over nothing and strangely defensive," Janet remarked. "That sounded so unlike you that I thought I'd ring and check how you are."

"Oh, I'm okay," Emma assured her. "Theresa and I had a difference of opinion about weaning but I don't suppose the situation will arise again."

"She's not the easiest person to deal with," Janet acknowledged. "She is so very opinionated - but she is always keen to help and she's very competent. Do you want me to take her off the rota?"

"I'm sure that's not necessary," Emma demurred. "That would seem very pointed and I don't want to hurt her feelings. The rota runs out soon and I'll be able to manage for myself after that."

CHAPTER 5

Charlie helped Emma in many different ways in the weeks after Sam's accident. They often prayed together and she was always available to sustain Emma as she coped with the incompetence and insensitivity of organisations, who could not seem to understand Emma's circumstances. One organisation insisted, for example, that they could only speak to the account holder, despite having already been formally notified that Sam, the account holder, was dead. Another wrote in reply to Emma's letter notifying them of Sam's death, as follows:

> *'Mr. S. Barton etc.*
> *Dear Mr. Barton,*
> *Thank you for your letter of 25th April. Having carefully considered your request, we are writing to confirm termination of your membership with immediate effect.*
> *Yours sincerely etc.'*

Charlie exhaled derisively when she read it.

"'Carefully considered'!" she repeated with scorn. "If they'd carefully considered your request they'd know better than to address the letter to Sam, for a start!"

Emma grimaced in agreement. Each letter and email

addressed to Sam aggravated the wounds of grief and loneliness, and Charlie's reaction was a balm to her distress. Emma tried very hard not to burden her friend too often with her problems as she was very conscious that Charlie had her own life to lead. Besides, she thought that Ed had already been astonishingly patient and generous in releasing his wife to help Emma on a couple of occasions at weekends, while he looked after Dan, and she did not want to abuse his kindness by taking up too much of her time and attention.

When the rota for meals came to an end, Janet asked whether Emma would like any ongoing assistance but, despite feeling that she was still operating through a fog which clouded many of her thoughts, Emma was eager to manage by herself. She felt a pressing need to prove to herself that she could cope without regular help in order to begin to believe that she was going to be able to survive in the long term as a single parent.

Her financial situation was no longer a major concern. Emma had learnt that Sam's savings amounted to what seemed a quite astonishing sum. He had also taken out life insurance shortly after their marriage and the pay-out from that would be significant. The necessary paperwork had been submitted to the insurance company but Emma guessed that the processes within such organisations might well be slow and that it was likely to be some time before the money reached her. It was not a matter of anxiety. Emma fully intended to reinvest the sum for the future benefit of the twins as soon as probate was complete.

She had made careful calculations and would certainly have enough to live on for the next five years, at least, and she supposed that, once Millie and Joel were at school, she could look for work and earn her own income.

Scarcely had she begun to settle into some kind of independent routine than the news reached her that Sam's body could at last be released.

Having been left in uncertainty for several weeks, it was a great relief to be able to finalise arrangements for the short cremation service and subsequent service of thanksgiving at their church, St Anthony's. Most of the details had already been agreed with Michael and the date was soon settled: Thursday the nineteenth of May. Again Charlie was ready with sympathy and support, and generously offered to help in ensuring that the necessary information was disseminated to all who might be interested.

Emma's mother advised her daughter by return that she would be arriving on the Wednesday morning and would require collecting from the airport.

Torn between relief at the prospect of her mother's presence and annoyance at the style of her communication, Emma loaded the twins into the car for the drive to Gatwick on Wednesday with mixed emotions of anticipation, apprehension and rising stress. She offered up a quick prayer for an uneventful journey and for the twins to stay quiet during the trip. She knew from past experience that it was almost impossible to drive with proper concentration if the babies were screaming in the back of the car.

The outward journey was accomplished without much trouble, the only excitement being a minor incident which closed one lane of the motorway; but as the midmorning traffic was not heavy the delay was minimal and Emma was at the airport in good time before her mother was due to arrive. Millie and Joel were strapped into their double buggy and, in order to avoid testing their patience too far, Emma wheeled them around for a while before taking up her position at the designated meeting point and endeavouring to keep a look out amidst the milling throng.

When her mother came into view, marching purposefully through the mêlée with her battered and utilitarian travel bag, her chin jutting authoritatively as she negotiated the obstacles in her path and scanned the crowd for the first sight of her daughter, Emma felt a relaxation of the tension inside her and an unaccustomed degree of affection. The relief at the prospect of having a more senior family member with whom to share some of her burdens was, however, short-lived.

Having greeted her daughter affectionately enough and briefly surveyed the twins, Dorothy Mann commented unfavourably on the temperature, the flight attendants and her fellow travellers, and expressed a desire for a revivifying coffee. Emma obligingly turned the buggy and led the way towards one of the various refreshment outlets, only to have her mother announce that the prices were ridiculously inflated and that she had no intention of pandering to such blatant greed.

"I'll pay," Emma offered, wanting to get back to the car.

"Nonsense. You won't be able to waste your money like that now you're on your own. Let's look somewhere else."

By the time Dorothy had visited and rejected every possible source of coffee at the airport, Emma was beginning to lose patience and so were Millie and Joel. As Dorothy abandoned her search for a reasonably-priced cup of coffee, the twins began to grumble; and on the way back to the car, the volume of Joel's display of displeasure steadily increased.

After a while, Dorothy, whose lips had been pressed together in irritation, commanded her daughter to give the child a soother.

"I don't use them," Emma replied bluntly.

"Why ever not?"

"Like most things, there are pros and cons - and I've never really needed them."

"You could do with one right now. Why don't you like them?"

"I'd have to keep them sterilised; it's another thing to carry and keep an eye on; and I didn't want the twins to become dependent on them, because it might be hard to break the habit."

"You three all had them and it didn't do *you* any harm," her mother answered dismissively. "And you can't be ruled by fear of the future. God's in control, so step out in faith!"

Emma wondered why such an exhortation, with which she was in full agreement, should cause her such exasperation coming at such a moment; but she held her tongue, counted to ten and walked a little faster.

"How's Dad?" she asked, deliberately changing the subject.

"Very busy, as always – so many people need his expertise. What are you going to do with yourself with Sam gone?"

"Millie and Joel keep me pretty busy, and there's been a lot to sort out in recent weeks."

"Sam's affairs must be sorted by now, surely? I thought you said you'd had help with all that."

"People have been very kind but it's not that simple," Emma replied defensively.

"It sounds to me as though you're letting the task expand to fill the time available," her mother commented severely. "A common failing."

"There isn't much time available with twins to look after," Emma protested.

"There are lots of widows in Pokhara with many more than two children to care for; and they have none of your modern appliances to make life easier."

Again Emma bit her tongue and willed herself not to respond.

This pattern was repeated throughout the day. Emma had to endure helpful criticisms of her driving, her housekeeping and her routine, as well as more generally derogatory comments about the lifestyle and amenities enjoyed by the British and so taken for granted. Her mother also pointed out several improvements which could be made around the house and even moved one or two items of furniture to better locations.

By the time her brother arrived after dinner, Emma had reached the point where almost everything her mother did or said was an added irritant.

Emma was washing the dishes and her mother was drying up when the doorbell rang. Before Emma could wipe her hands and respond, her mother had laid down the tea towel and, without a word or glance, had moved to answer it. Such a characteristic usurpation of her role caused Emma to send up an arrow prayer for patience as she followed her mother into the hall.

Luke, who was three years older than Emma and

about eight inches taller, looked very much what he was: an up-and-coming businessman establishing a reputation for himself as a bright, young financier, likely to see great success both personally and for his company. He had the same curly, honey-gold hair as his younger sister but his was cropped ruthlessly short. His eyes were the same shade of grey-blue as hers but his gaze was much more steely and had been known to discomfit rivals and incompetent juniors most severely, whilst his nose was a beaked prow that gave his face a great deal of character and bore no resemblance to his sister's dainty little retroussé feature.

He greeted their mother with civil but guarded brevity; then he put her aside, abandoned his wheeled travel case, and gave Emma a hearty bear hug, thumping her encouragingly on the back and saying: "Hey, Sis! Good to see you. How are you?"

"Better," Emma conceded. "But dreading tomorrow."

"We'll look after you," he assured her breezily.

"Traditional Nepalese funeral ceremonies often last for three days or more," their mother informed them. "And then they'll have another three-day ceremony a year later."

"Viking longboat – that's the best idea," Luke said flippantly.

"If by that you mean putting the body in a boat, setting it on fire and launching it out to sea, that's pure myth," Dorothy retorted. "I don't believe any Viking was ever dispatched in that way. Besides which, it would be dangerous and probably illegal."

Luke rolled his eyes at his sister, but asked after his nephew and niece mildly enough.

"Come and meet them," said Emma and led the way

eagerly back to the kitchen where Millie and Joel were each secured in a bouncy chair and swatting experimentally at toys affixed in front of them.

"Well, don't dress them in yellow and green!" Luke teased. "Now how can I work out which is which?"

"Millie has more hair," his mother said instructively, again implicitly arrogating Emma's part.

"I suppose if one of them is going to be bald, it had better be the boy!"

Emma chuckled, but her mother pointed out unnecessarily that Joel's hair would soon grow.

"Would you like a drink?" Emma asked her brother.

"Black coffee, please."

While the kettle was heating up, Emma finished the washing up. It was fortunate that she stayed in the kitchen because, for some reason, the kettle did not switch itself off automatically once it had reached boiling point. It had happened once or twice before and Emma assumed that she had somehow splashed water on to the wrong part of the device, and thought no more about it.

Once he had finished his coffee, Luke went upstairs to make himself comfortable and then joined his family for the bath-time routine, which was certainly easier with the additional adults on hand, but was no quicker because Luke turned the whole enterprise into a game and had the twins constantly laughing and gurgling at his antics.

Having helped to get them dry and dressed, he sensibly offered to leave them to settle for the night without his unique assistance and heroically took Dorothy away with him on the pretext of needing some advice about the business which he had to transact while in the UK.

It may seem strange that so shrewd and censorious a lady should be so readily conned into compliance by her son but affection has frequently clouded even clearer judgement and the prospect of having her opinion sought was always a considerable inducement to one who had an opinion on everything.

Of course, she was perfectly willing to proffer guidance even when it had not been sought and, later that evening, seeing her daughter wrapping the gift she had bought to thank Charlie and Ed for all their recent support, Dorothy could not resist suggesting that Emma had been unduly extravagant and that friendship should not require repayment.

"It's not meant as payment. I just wanted to - to express my gratitude. They've been brilliant – and they have a toddler of their own to look after so it's been especially good of them to help out so much."

"If you must give something, a nominal gift would have been sufficient."

"But this bowl will be just right for their kitchen. It matches their tiles almost perfectly."

"You should avoid being overgenerous. Don't forget, money is the root of all evil," her mother said reprovingly. "And, as I keep telling you, you'll need to be more careful with your money now you're by yourself."

Recognising the anguish in his sister's face, Luke, who had been reclining at his ease in an old armchair in the corner, stood up and strolled over to the table where she was working. He delved into his jacket pocket with his right hand, drew out a roll of banknotes which he held out to Emma and remarked that he'd meant to hand it over at the end of his visit. "But you might as well have it now and - with any luck - we can change the subject - although it is the *love* of money that is the root of all evil. Anyway, there's plenty more where that came from so don't be shy of asking, little Sis."

"But you shouldn't," Emma protested.

"Yes, I should."

"I don't think -."

"*Don't* think. Give me your hand."

When Emma still held back, he took a firm hold of her hand, turned it over and pressed the roll of notes into it. She thanked him uncomfortably and tucked it hastily away, very conscious of their mother's silent disapprobation and careful to avoid any change of countenance which could be construed as triumphant.

At bedtime, when she took the roll out of her pocket and counted it, she realised that her brother had casually handed over five hundred pounds in crisp twenty pound notes.

Endeavouring to express her gratitude to Luke over breakfast the following morning, she found him uninterested and determined to change the subject. As she had a great deal on her mind, she did not pursue the topic, only resolving to write and thank him properly at some point so that she could properly record her appreciation without being cut short.

Meanwhile, Luke made a jocular reference to the twins being a very effective alarm clock and remarked that he hoped he had not disturbed anyone by occupying the bathroom at an early hour. "I thought I'd get on and get out of the way," he explained. "By the way, either I am weaker than I knew or your bathroom tap has a permanent drip."

"Yes, it's a bit of a nuisance," agreed Emma absent-mindedly, pushing the muesli round in her bowl. "I think the washer is worn. Sam was planning to replace it sometime."

"Remember how lucky you are to have hot and cold running water piped to the house," her mother told her. "Many households in Nepal don't have that luxury."

Luke exhaled in exasperation. "If I was the DIY type, I'd have a look at it," he said to his sister. "But as it is, I'd definitely do more harm than good. Do you know anyone who could help?"

"I might be able to ask Ed," Emma replied doubtfully.

"You ought to find out whether there's someone at church who's a proper handyman," her mother advised. "There'll be all sorts of little jobs that you need help with now Sam's gone, and you don't want to pay if you don't have to."

Emma wished her mother would not remind her so frequently of her widowhood but she said nothing. On this day of all days, she was unlikely to forget her tragedy for long so she could hardly blame her mother for bringing it to mind. Luke caught her eye and grimaced, before directing her attention to her breakfast and suggesting that her cereal would be dizzy.

Forcing herself to eat a few mouthfuls, Emma tried not to dwell on what lay ahead over the next few hours. She prayed that she would survive the formalities without breaking down completely or doing something foolish or embarrassing to others. She wanted everything to go well so as to honour Sam's memory, although she knew that none of it would matter to him anymore: he was at home with the Lord. It was she who had to face an uncertain future in a bleak life of struggle and regret.

CHAPTER 6

Two of the older ladies in the church family had been deputed to look after the twins for the duration of the morning cremation service, which was attended only by relatives and a few close friends.

Before the service, Emma forced herself to take the trouble to speak to Sam's elderly great aunts and his cousin, who had come from some distance. Each of them turned out to have attended more out of curiosity than from respect for Sam's memory. They were inconsiderately garrulous and seemingly oblivious to her grief and Emma struggled to respond suitably.

Thus she was initially relieved when the vicar took her aside just before he began the service, to apologise for Janet's absence. "She had intended to come this morning because she was planning to help Doreen with the babysitting this afternoon, but I'm afraid she has a migraine. She's very sorry not be here."

"How unpleasant for her," Emma responded automatically, barely able to give any attention to what he was saying. "I hope she'll be better soon."

"I'm sure she will," Michael said comfortably. "She suffers with migraines from time to time but they usually only last a day or two. And don't worry about this afternoon.

As soon as she realised the migraine was coming on, Janet phoned Doreen and asked her to find someone else to help, so it's all sorted."

Emma thanked him mechanically and slid into a seat next to her mother. She took a deep breath as if to brace herself, and focussed all her thoughts on the words of the short service. Her eyes prickled and her throat closed repeatedly as she listened, but she fought down her tears until the words of the Committal were declared by Michael:

> We have entrusted our brother Samuel to God's mercy, and we now commit his body to be cremated: earth to earth, ashes to ashes, dust to dust: in sure and certain hope of the resurrection to eternal life through our Lord Jesus Christ, who will transform our frail bodies that they may be conformed to his glorious body, who died, was buried, and rose again for us. To him be glory for ever.

Then there was no possibility of suppressing her anguish or holding back the tears.

At this point, her mother came into her own. She handed Emma a clean handkerchief and laid an arm briefly across her shoulders, patting her bracingly and telling her quietly that it would all be over soon.

Once the service concluded she shepherded Emma away as soon as she could politely do so and, having deposited her silently weeping daughter in the back seat of the car with instructions to Luke to keep an eye on her, she took over the management of the event and the organisation of transport back to Emma's house, where they were all to have lunch.

Luke had scarcely had time to join Emma in the car and say gently, "Poor Sis!" as he reached out to comfort her, when their sister, Rachel opened the car door and bent down to lean in.

"Oh Emma," said Rachel hurriedly, plainly embarrassed by her sister's distress and unwilling to look directly at her. "I'm glad I've caught you. I just wanted to let you know that Harry and I'll have to hurry away at the end of the thanksgiving service later. I have to be back in time to pick the children up from school."

Luke frowned at his older sister. "Couldn't other parents help out?"

"I didn't ask. Well, Harry needs to get back for a business call anyway. Besides, if someone else picks the children up, they'll want to know why; and we haven't told them about Uncle Sam yet. They're too young to deal with that kind of thing – Clemmie especially. It's important to shield them from unpleasantness for as long as possible."

"For pity's sake, Rachel!" Luke protested irritably. "Listen to yourself! Millie and Joel are only a few months old and they've lost their *father*: how are *they* going to be shielded from unpleasantness?"

"But that's unavoidable," Rachel pointed out. "And they're too young to know anything about it."

"Then think how Emma might be feeling, for once," Luke advised. "Instead of directing all your thoughts and cares towards your sheltered and indulged offspring."

"You'll be exactly the same if you ever have children of your own," Rachel replied defensively.

"Doubt it."

"I guess we'll never know," Rachel jibed. "The way you're going, you're unlikely to have any."

"Stop it!" Please stop it," Emma begged.

"Very well!" said Rachel huffily. "I'm going to find Harry." She turned and stalked away on her high heels.

"Sorry, Sis," Luke offered contritely. "She drives me up the wall but I shouldn't retaliate."

"It's alright. She drives me up the wall too."

"But you're too kind to respond. I do pray for patience, but it's not my forte."

"I'm not patient really – not inside," Emma confessed. "Inside, I'm often screaming with annoyance, but somehow I prefer to keep it to myself – unless I'm really pushed beyond breaking point."

"I'll watch out for that then!" Luke smiled.

Emma managed a half-smile in return and was able to wipe her eyes and blow her nose, sitting up straighter and composing herself, so that when her mother joined them in the car, she was pleased to commend Luke for his care.

"We ought to get back to Emma's house fairly speedily," she added briskly. "The babies will need feeding and we have to deal with lunch and get back to St Anthony's by two thirty. Let's press on."

The meal was a subdued affair, but, under their mother's eagle eye and authoritative directions, Luke and Rachel set aside their differences and did what they could to be helpful in laying and clearing the table, whilst others chatted amongst themselves and Harry occupied himself in a corner with his smartphone.

"He always has so many emails," Rachel explained

excusingly. "He has to keep on top of them almost constantly."

Luke raised his eyebrows heavenward but refrained from comment. Emma knew that he also had an international role with a constant stream of emails but that he had sufficient self-discipline to avoid looking at them at a time like this.

"If it's not work," Rachel went on, oblivious to her brother's disapproval, "it'll be emails from his golf club. He's been asked to take on the role of treasurer, which is a great honour. Of course, he doesn't really have time, but there are quite a lot of local big shots at the club and it might be very useful to get to know them better. You can never tell when that kind of connection might come in handy. It's the same with the schools we've chosen. Some of the parents are multi-millionaires with houses in Spain and that kind of thing – just the sort of friendships you want your children to make – free holidays and lots of other advantages."

"I think I want my children to make friendships based on character and commonality, not on material benefits," Emma remarked.

"Oh, yes," Rachel said indifferently. "But if you can have material benefits as well, who's complaining?"

After the meal, Emma went upstairs to feed and change the twins. Just as she was finishing, her mother came to find her, to tell her that the second pair of babysitters had arrived.

"I'll be down soon," Emma said, busy with the fastenings on Millie's vest, and reluctant to return to the formal duties of the day.

"I'll make them a cup of tea," her mother said. "But don't be long now. We'll need to set off for the church soon."

After her mother had disappeared downstairs, Emma

lingered over clothing the twins and was still playing with Joel on the changing mat when Luke knocked and popped his head around the door to deliver a message from their mother. "She says we ought to be leaving," he reported. "She's standing in the hall with her coat on, even though there's still more than half an hour before the service starts. She's sent everyone else off already so you'd better come down. Let me carry one of these little rascals."

He scooped Millie up as he spoke and bore her away chuckling. Emma followed more slowly with Joel, holding him to her for comfort and reassurance and, as soon as she appeared round the corner of the stairs, her mother began exhorting her to hurry.

Emma focussed her gaze on the scene below and saw that the two babysitters were also waiting in the hall, that Luke was already handing Millie over to Doreen Carr and that the other face looking up at her belonged to Theresa Halton. She halted momentarily on the quarter space in dismay and then, since there was no help for it, continued downstairs. She remembered Michael's earlier explanation and supposed that Doreen had no reason to know that, after her last visit, Emma would have preferred almost anyone other than Theresa to be involved. However, it was impossible to say as much now. Instead, she civilly thanked the ladies for coming to look after the twins and added firmly. "They've just been fed, so there'll be no need to give them anything to eat or drink. Let me just show you where everything is."

"I think I know my way around," Theresa replied confidently. "Your mother wants to leave. Don't let us delay you."

"Come *on*, Emma!" her mother urged.

So she handed Joel over with great reluctance and, as Luke helped her into her coat, she reminded the ladies that the twins would not need feeding. "They'll probably settle to sleep for a while," she added hopefully.

"Just leave it to us. We've looked after plenty of babies between us," Theresa responded. Her assurance grated, but Emma was chivvied away by her mother and found herself on the way to the church before she could think.

Not that her thoughts were at all coherent even then. They flitted from one anxiety to another and all she could do was pray silently for the strength to get through the afternoon. It was a grey day of heavy cloud and persistent mizzle and the view from the car window was a depressing one, but Emma did not notice. Her thoughts were all turned inwards and her companions' conversation flowed around her without once penetrating her consciousness.

Inevitably, they arrived at the church very early and Emma had to muster up the courage to speak to well-wishers as they waited. Charlie and Ed soon appeared with Dan, and Emma was very glad to see them and to relax her guard a little, although Rachel no doubt disapproved of exposing a young child to such a traumatic experience.

It dawned on Emma that, in the needless rush, she had forgotten the present she had chosen and wrapped so carefully for Charlie and Ed. She would have to find another opportunity to hand it over.

By the time the service began, the church was almost full. There was plenty of support from their church family and many of Sam's friends and work colleagues had come to pay their last respects, while a number of Emma's friends also attended in sympathy and support.

Much of the afternoon passed for Emma as if it were some kind of performance viewed from a great distance. She was so focussed on endeavouring to negotiate the public ceremony acceptably that she played her part automatically, whilst often almost entirely divorced from the tangible realities of the proceedings. She did not even realise that the organist was lacking in expertise or that the church was cold, until her mother pointed out these inadequacies later.

Only a few things stood out in the press of amorphous impressions and unremembered faces. One was the singing of Townend and Getty's worship song 'In Christ alone my hope is found' at the end of the service. It pierced her abstraction with the vivid memory of singing it, together with Sam and their guests, on their wedding day two years ago. All her bitter regrets threatened to overwhelm her but she had cried so much that morning and this time she ruthlessly thrust the memory back down into the recesses of her mind.

Another brief interlude of clarity occurred during the informal gathering for refreshments after the service. She had been engaged in a stilted conversation with one of Sam's work colleagues, who had been assuring her with clumsy awkwardness that Sam had been so proud of his wife and ecstatically happy at the birth of the twins. She brought the exchange to what she hoped was a courteous conclusion and turned away, only to realise that Nick was standing at her shoulder, waiting to speak to her. He was accompanied by a tall, slender young lady with a fall of glossy brown, shoulder-length hair and large dark eyes, her hand resting affectionately in the crook of his elbow.

Anger welled up in Emma, briefly dispelling the barriers she had erected between herself and the rest of the world. Nick might look very smart in his dark suit and with his attractive girlfriend on his arm, but he could have no possible business being there. He had never known Sam and he certainly could not regard himself as a friend of *hers*.

He said something which she did not quite catch, so preoccupied was she with her own burgeoning resentment, and just as she began to focus he added, "This is Penny."

Emma nodded at the girl unsmilingly.

"It's good to meet you at last," Penny said with shy eagerness. "I've heard so much about you. I'm so - so sorry for your loss."

Perhaps Nick sensed Emma's silent antagonism because he very simply added a brief sentence expressing his sympathy and took his leave.

Emma watched Penny put her arm around him as they walked away. She thought bitterly of her own loneliness. Now that Sam was gone, there was no one to provide company or comfort, no one to share her moments of sadness or joy, no one to take an interest in what became of her and the children.

In that slough of deep self-pity, Charlie found her and, tucking her hand around Emma's arm, said encouragingly, "You're amazing. Everyone's been saying how well you've done today."

"Charlie," Emma confessed desperately, with a tremor in her voice. "I'm *not* amazing. I – I can't manage any longer. I just want to leave and get home to the twins." A sob escaped her.

Looking at Emma's white face, Charlie guessed that she was close to collapse.

"Come with me," she said firmly. "Let's find your family." Keeping hold of her friend's arm as if the contact might lend her strength, Charlie steered her purposefully through the press of people until they encountered Luke, who summed up the situation with a glance, thanked Charlotte for her help and, putting an arm round his sister, led her away to the car.

"I'm taking you home," he told her. "Wait here. I'll let Mum know or we'll never hear the last of it."

He opened the door and she got in and sat huddled in the passenger seat, shaking with stress and grief.

Time passed.

Her shivering gradually subsided. Eventually, Luke returned with Dorothy and they set off.

Luke drove in sympathetic silence, but silence was not Dorothy's natural metier and she soon began to speak of the day, reviewing every aspect of the service. "I thanked the vicar for you before I left," she remarked at one point. "And - as I told him - it was not his fault that the organist had a most peculiar sense of rhythm and no idea how to mark the start of each verse."

Emma had recovered enough to hear what her mother was saying but she had no energy to protest at such heavy-handed tactlessness. She was longing get home, to hold the twins close and to shut out the rest of the world and even her own thoughts – especially her own thoughts.

"I do think they might have had the heating on,"

Dorothy continued. "It was very chilly in church. Nearly everyone kept their coats on. And that toddler – Daniel, was it? – what was he doing at the service? Such a distraction to the rest of us."

"He was very good," Luke pointed out. "Sat quietly most of the time with books and toys and a pack of raisins."

"Most of which ended up on the floor – and *after* the service -."

As soon as the car pulled up outside her trim little house, Emma scrambled out and hurried up the short path, fishing her key out as she went. Letting herself in and leaving the front door ajar for her mother and brother to follow, she looked hastily into the sitting room. Finding it empty, she went on through to the kitchen where she found Doreen and Theresa sitting and chatting at the table with cups of tea, while the twins played in their bouncy chairs.

At first glance the scene looked idyllic and Emma had just begun to breathe a sigh of relief when she realised that Joel was clutching a set of keys, which he was endeavouring to get into his mouth but was in more danger of poking into his eye instead. Quick as a flash, she whisked over and prised the keys from his tenacious little fist, quickly replacing them with a safe plastic toy. However, he was not impressed by this arbitrary interference and made his annoyance known.

"Poor chap," remarked Theresa. "He was having such fun with my keys. Babies always love them, you know. They're shiny and jangly and cool for sore gums."

"Not very hygienic though," Emma pointed out, keeping a tight rein on her temper. "And definitely not great if they jab themselves in the eye with them."

She picked Joel out of his seat as she spoke and distracted

him from his displeasure by lifting him high over her head and swinging him back down again.

Luke and their mother had now joined them and Doreen got to her feet saying that they had better be going.

"I'll just wash these cups for you," Theresa said. "It'll save you a job."

She trod heavily over to the sink, rinsed the cups briefly under the cold tap and propped them on the draining rack, then picked up the washing-up sponge, wiped a tea ring off the work surface, bent down to wipe a splash off the floor with the same sponge, and returned it to the draining rack, where it came to rest against one of the cups.

Holding Joel snuggled against her neck, Emma watched in horrified distaste and could barely wait to see the two ladies safely out of the front door before handing Joel to her brother and rapidly relegating the sponge to the floor-cleaning bucket under the sink, loading the two cups into the dishwasher and disinfecting the draining rack, putting the disinfectant back in the cupboard and shutting the door with unnecessary vigour.

"What's all the fuss about?" asked her mother.

"That woman," returned Emma, with a sob, "is the most interfering, opinionated woman I have ever met!"

"You're over-reacting."

"Mum!" Luke said warningly.

"I am *not* over-reacting," Emma stated furiously, dashing away a tear. "She has *no* idea of cleanliness or of child safety. I don't want her in my house ever again!"

"You'll be glad of her help one day," her mother predicted.

"I would not trust her within *yards* of my babies after the way she's behaved."

"Babies are tougher than you think," her mother told her. "Here in the West, they're hugely over protected. In Nepal, they survive with far less mollycoddling."

"Remind us how infant mortality rates compare between Britain and Nepal," Luke interposed smoothly.

"I don't only want my children to *survive*," Emma added vehemently. "I want them to *thrive*."

As Millie was demanding attention, Emma was glad to be able to walk away from the debate and attend to her little daughter, but Luke and their mother continued to thrash out their difference of opinion for some time.

CHAPTER 7

After an early evening meal, Luke had to take his leave. He was due at a meeting in Edinburgh first thing the following morning and had arranged to travel north overnight. He disappeared upstairs and came down a short while later with his travel case. Having given each of the twins a farewell tickle, he stooped to kiss his mother dutifully and then hugged his sister warmly, reminding her quietly to let him know if she needed anything.

"Thank you," Emma said, with real gratitude. "Thank you so much for the gift – and everything; and thank you for coming. It's been great to have your support."

"No worries," he replied cheerfully. "Don't thank me. I got to speak to a very pretty girl after the service. I should be thanking you!"

On which facetious note, he made his exit, leaving Emma to try to deflect her mother's criticisms. To her accusation that Luke was becoming increasingly selfish, Emma reminded her of his generosity in paying her air fare and in handing over a very sizeable gift, but her mother rejected this defence, saying that he would barely notice parting with those sorts of sums. "He has settled into a way of life which means that he need only ever consider himself. His whole life is devoted to making more money for himself and his employers. It is a far from admirable goal and hardly suggests Christian values."

"He is presumably, like all of us, a work in progress," Emma replied. "I know he's still reading his Bible and praying, so he hasn't abandoned Christianity."

"In a work environment where people are motivated solely by profit, I fear that he can only drift further from his upbringing."

"Perhaps he can be an influence for good in his workplace. Any environment must benefit from having Christians in the mix to be salt and light."

"Without support, he won't achieve much. He needs a good church and Christian friends – or he needs to find a nice Christian girl to marry - but whenever I try to talk to him about it, he refuses to be serious."

"Maybe he thinks that, at nearly thirty years old, he's old enough to look after himself."

"If he honoured his parents more, he'd appreciate our concern. As it is, I wonder whether he'll always be restless and self-seeking."

"Perhaps it depends what God wants him to do with his life," Emma replied lightly, and quoted: "*For I know the plans I have for you,' declares the Lord. 'Plans to prosper you and not to harm you, plans to give you hope and a future.'* That came up in my Bible reading notes this morning."

"You can't just pluck quotes out of context," her mother rebuked her. "Anyway, I've always hoped my children would settle down, get married and have a family."

"I know, but it's not always a recipe for happiness," Emma pointed out.

"Mmm," her mother sniffed and, although she had the

grace to look a little awkward, she could not resist adding, "You do seem to attract disaster. You've lost Sam after only a couple of years of marriage – and I haven't forgotten that dreadful relationship you had when you were at university. That's certainly not what I want for Luke – but I would like him to think about it seriously for once. The Lord helps those who help themselves."

"I don't think that's even from the Bible," Emma objected with great restraint.

"You're as bad as your brother – no respect for your elders. Your lack of appreciation for the time those two ladies gave up this afternoon is a good example."

"I thanked them more than once."

"But you didn't mean it, did you? I saw the way you reacted after they'd gone."

"At least I waited till they'd gone."

"There was no need to react like that at all."

"You can't be suggesting that I have to show respect for my elders by allowing them to take risks with my children that I would never take myself. That's ridiculous!"

"You're overwrought," her mother said reprovingly. "Let's get the twins upstairs for their bath."

Emma suspected that her mother was side-stepping the issue because she had no good answer to the challenge; but she would never be brought to admit as much and Emma was glad to abandon the discussion and turn her thoughts to Mille and Joel.

The rest of the evening passed harmoniously enough, and Emma was too tired to stay up long after the twins were asleep.

Waking early the following morning, Emma reviewed

her plans for the day. Recalling from critical comments on previous visits that, unconvinced by any environmental arguments, her mother disapproved of the modern tendency of so many Westerners to have their supermarket shopping delivered to their door, Emma had not placed an online order that week and intended to take her mother to the local supermarket and fill the morning by shopping for food and, perhaps, if her mother could be brought to overlook the cost, stopping for a drink in the café.

If the weather was dry, they could perhaps go to the park in the afternoon, or, if her mother was prepared to keep an eye on the twins, she could tackle some of the rather overdue tasks around the garden. They only had the one day to occupy, as her mother was booked on a flight back to Nepal at Saturday lunchtime and Emma thought that was probably a good thing. It was undoubtedly helpful to have another adult to take a turn with Millie and Joel, but the frequent exasperation engendered by her mother's attitudes made her feel that the help was sometimes dearly bought.

In the event, the weather was worse than the previous day. Rain showers fell from a dark grey sky at intervals throughout the morning and by the time Emma had negotiated the heavy traffic, the busy car park, the crowded supermarket and the long and jaded queues of shoppers, she felt no inclination to test her mother's reaction to the prices in the supermarket coffee shop.

Joining the line of cars waiting to leave the car park, Emma commented without reflection on the inescapable effect of rain on the number of cars on the road. Her mother seized the opportunity to describe the monsoon rains in Nepal and to explain that the majority of households there did not have a car. "Most of them couldn't afford such a luxury. Of course, roads are sometimes impassable anyway because of mudslides and so on. Count your blessings."

"Oh, I do," Emma replied, quelled, and drove on in silence.

The continuing wet weather rendered it impossible to carry out either of the plans Emma had devised for the afternoon and her mother announced over lunch that she would rather like to take the opportunity to catch up with an old friend who lived in Epsom. "I spoke to Mollie this morning and told her I'm only around this afternoon and, in order to save you another drive, she suggested that she could come over here for afternoon tea. That'll be alright, won't it? I said it would be fine."

"If I say it's not convenient, what will you do?"

"Phone her back and offer to meet somewhere else. But you're not doing anything else, are you?"

"No," Emma replied, resigning herself to the inevitable.

Although Mollie was pleased to fuss over the babies for a little while and to have a cuddle with each of them, she was plainly more interested in chatting to Dorothy and in talking about her own family.

Emma put the kettle on and noticed that, once more, it failed to switch itself off. "I really must be more careful when I top it up," she thought to herself, although she was a little puzzled because she did not think she had filled the kettle unduly vigorously. However, it seemed to function properly most of the time, so she assumed there could be nothing significant wrong with it.

Once she had made a pot of tea and supplied a plate of biscuits, Emma left the older ladies to chat in the sitting room and played with the twins in the kitchen, whilst intermittently making preparations for the evening meal. By the time her mother had had enough of sociability and had waved Mollie goodbye, Emma had washed and chopped the vegetables, prepared a chicken casserole and put it in the oven to cook.

"Something smells appetising," her mother commented guardedly as she entered the kitchen. "Is it chicken?"

Emma nodded silently.

"That will be a treat. Meat consumption is much lower in Nepal than it is here and the availability and the price of chicken in Pokhara have fluctuated widely in recent years with outbreaks of avian flu and the resultant culls. Has it had much impact in the UK?" her mother asked.

"Not that I've noticed. There was some concern when it first hit the headlines but nothing much since then."

They kept their conversation to similarly neutral topics as much as possible and, by this means, were able to get through the evening without any major differences of opinion.

After a night of heavy rain, Saturday dawned with blue skies and bright sunshine. As the time for her mother's departure drew near, Emma found that she was better able to appreciate her assistance and to tolerate her idiosyncrasies, which made an affectionate and grateful parting more natural and genuine.

Having dropped her mother off at the airport mid-morning, Emma called on Charlotte, to deliver the present she had forgotten on Thursday. There was a convenient parking space available right outside Charlie's house, so Emma left the sleeping twins in their car seats and carried the parcel with her to the front door, intending to hand it over with a few words of thanks and head home. However, she had not considered that Ed would not be at work on a Saturday and was rather caught off guard when he answered the door.

She tried self-consciously to hand over her gift and he promptly invited her in.

"Charlie's out in the back garden with Dan," he said cheerfully. "Come through and say hello."

"I don't want to interrupt," she objected.

"You won't. You can't run off without seeing Charlie. She'd be very disappointed."

"The twins are asleep in the car," she excused herself, feeling that she had imposed on Charlie and Ed more than enough, but he still pressed her to step inside and offered to help fetch the twins in their car seats so as not to disturb them.

Aware of a great disinclination to return to her empty house, Emma allowed herself to be persuaded.

The back garden of Ed and Charlie's house was not large and comprised a tidy patio with a table and four chairs and some colourful tubs, and a neat lawn surrounded by a narrow flower border and a wire fence. Charlie was hanging clothes out on the washing line while Dan knelt by a small sandpit on the patio, busy with a toy digger.

As soon as Charlie saw her friend, she abandoned the washing and came over to greet her. She unwrapped the present, exclaimed delightedly at the contents and showed the bowl to her husband so that he could also admire it.

"It'll look great in our kitchen," she said enthusiastically.

"How clever of you to find something that goes so well with our tiles."

"When I saw it in the shop, I immediately thought of your tiles. It's to say thank you to you both for all your help and support."

"There was no need to do that, but I love it. I'm going to take it inside and admire it in its proper setting," Charlie announced. "Would you like a coffee?"

"I don't want to get in the way."

"Don't be silly. We'd have a drink soon anyway."

"Then I'd love one. Shall I finish hanging up the washing for you?"

"Why don't I deal with the washing?" Ed suggested. "Perhaps you could keep an eye on Dan."

So Emma sat at the patio table in the bright May sunshine, with a sleeping twin on either side of her in their car seats, and watched Dan busily moving sand around with his little yellow digger in an incomprehensible but very purposeful way.

Ed soon finished hanging the washing out and then Charlie returned with a tray of drinks and a plate of shortbread and they all sat at the table to enjoy the refreshments together. Even Dan abandoned his mysterious sand manoeuvres when he realised that juice and biscuits were on offer.

This brief moment of sun-warmed leisure was interrupted by the ringing of the telephone, and Ed hauled himself reluctantly out of his chair and went indoors to answer it. Returning a short while later, he responded to his wife's enquiring look by explaining that it had been Nick on the phone.

"He was calling because he's looked out that set of books he mentioned and he was wondering when to drop them over here. Now he's moved in with Penny in Hither Green, he's probably only about fifteen miles away, but it's not a quick drive. Anyway, I suggested that they come round for lunch sometime - I thought it'd be good to get to know Penny a bit better. He's going to find out which Saturdays suit her and get back to us."

"That'd be nice," Charlie agreed, and then turned the subject. "Your brother was helpful on Thursday." she remarked to Emma. "He was very quick to come to your aid at the end of the afternoon."

"Yes, he's great. He was impressed with Dan, by the way. He commented on how well behaved he'd been at the service; which he was – very good and quiet."

"He's usually alright if he has plenty of amusements," Charlie said, pleased.

"And raisins!" Ed added with a slow smile. "Bribery and corruption works every time."

Emma did not forget what she had heard about Nick and Penny. Later, when she had leisure to consider it more fully, her chief emotion was a melancholy sense of isolation. Public opinion all seemed to point to the notion that the ideal goal was to be in a relationship, to be a couple. Most of her friends and acquaintances were paired off and just beginning to enjoy life as couples – as Nick and Penny now were – but, for herself, that had been cut short and she was alone again in a world of couples.

She wondered a little at Nick's lack of principle. He had spoken of becoming a minister and yet he was living with a girl he had not married. However, she knew that there were many who would think he was doing nothing reprehensible, particularly if he intended to marry Penny one day. She recalled that he had seemed to have very strong principles when she had known him six years ago, but when he had broken off their relationship with a brief text, he had demonstrated his cowardice. If Penny was eager for them to live together perhaps he lacked the moral courage to resist.

CHAPTER 8

Having moved her furniture back to the locations she preferred, in deliberate defiance of her mother's recommendation, and having written to thank her brother, Luke, as she had resolved to do, Emma tried to put the memory of the last few weeks behind her. Life settled into some kind of routine as the days and weeks passed, and the haze of exhaustion slowly began to lift, although Millie and Joel continued to occupy much of Emma's time and thoughts. They gradually slept more reliably through the night, they learnt to roll over and to reach for their own feet. They made noises that were beginning to sound to a fond mother a little like speech and they would take their weight on their own legs when she danced them on her lap, so that she suspected they were getting into training for standing and walking.

She desperately longed for someone with whom to share the voyage of discovery that is parenthood, to discuss the joys and concerns, the incremental steps of progress and development. She missed Sam's warm support, encouragement and admiration and, most of all, she missed the ongoing close companionship, the sense that someone else was interested in her day-to-day experiences, the little details of her life, and cared as much as she did about the twins.

Her parents phoned weekly with exhortations and admonitions. Emma understood that they were genuinely concerned for her welfare, but she wished they had a more kindly way of showing it. Luke kept in occasional contact, chiefly by email, and Rachel sent infrequent texts.

Charlie made a commitment to meet up with her friend most weeks, sometimes for lunch or coffee and sometimes to take Dan to feed the ducks in the park or go on the swings, while Millie and Joel watched from their buggy. She also supplied occasional helpings of homemade pasta bake or stew to ensure that Emma could have an easy, nutritious meal once in a while. She suspected, quite rightly, that although Emma knew she had to eat sensibly, there would be days when she would simply lack the time and energy to feed herself properly.

Emma's church family continued to be a source of friendship and encouragement. She started attending a mums and toddlers group they ran on a Wednesday morning in term time, where Janet kept a special eye out for her, and she was also a regular at the Monday morning women's Bible study group which provided a wonderful crèche for all the youngsters. Emma was happy to make use of the crèche once she had established that Theresa Halton was not one of the team of helpers. Fortunately, Theresa always took the train over to Dorking on a Monday and Wednesday to help in her daughter's shop.

It proved impossible, however, to avoid Theresa altogether. Every so often she would call on Emma with her fat, wheezy dog and an offering of food or some household item such as soap or kitchen roll. Even if Emma was out, these donations would be left in an old plastic bag by her front door with an explanatory note. Her home-cooked gifts were often as unsavoury as her original box of mince had been and Emma reluctantly wasted many of them; her other handouts were unashamedly bought from the end-of-line, short-date selection at the supermarket.

Emma tried to tell her that she was capable of cooking her own meals and that she was not in financial difficulties, but Theresa would not listen or did not want to hear. Emma was too polite to decline the gifts and even occasionally felt obliged to gratify Theresa by inviting her in for a cup of tea, although she took care never to leave Theresa alone with the twins and watched her carefully to ensure that no further health and safety breaches could occur.

One hot Saturday afternoon in late June, when the twins were almost five months old, Emma came in from the back garden to answer a ring on the door bell and found Theresa and her labrador standing there with the customary, shabby, carrier bag.

"Hello, dear. I've brought you some bananas."

"Oh, er, thank you," Emma said reluctantly.

Theresa held the plastic bag out to her expectantly so Emma felt obliged to take it.

"They're a bit soft," Theresa explained. "But that'll be fine for mashing up for the babies."

"They're not on solid food yet."

"Still not? That's very odd. Perhaps these would be a good thing to start them on then. Otherwise, you can always eat them yourself - very high in nutrients, ripe bananas."

"I know."

"Could I ask a favour, dear? Poor old Barley has had a long walk on a hot day and could do with a bowl of water. Could we come in for a mo so she can have a drink?"

"Of course. Come through to the kitchen," Emma replied courteously, although she was longing to get back to the weeding that she had started when Millie and Joel had dosed off in the playpen in the shady corner of the lawn after lunch. She opened the door wide to let Theresa and her dog past and followed them into the kitchen, asking politely whether Theresa would also like a drink.

"I wouldn't say no to a cup of tea, if you're making one," she responded predictably.

Emma had not planned to make one just yet, but there was no possible civil reply to such a remark other than to oblige, and Emma put the plastic bag on the table and went and flicked the kettle on, saying, "I'll just check on the twins. They're out in the garden. I'll be back in a moment."

Barley trailed after her, tugging at her lead, and Theresa allowed herself to be pulled out into the back garden.

Millie and Joel were still asleep but Emma watched warily as Barley headed towards the playpen and sniffed all round it, before uttering a deep bark and moving as swiftly as she could tug her owner towards the hedge at the foot of the garden. A sound of scrabbling paws came from the far side of the hedge, followed by some frenzied yelping, and in seconds the air was filled with barking and growling. Barley's efforts to reach the source of the yelping eventually dragged her lead out of Theresa's hands and she ran heavily up and down the hedgerow in great excitement, despite Theresa's repeated forceful commands to come to heel.

Into this scene of insubordination there burst a few

seconds later a small terrier, yapping and wagging its tail, and racing off up the lawn at high speed to explore this newfound space. Barley lolloped after it and the noise of the chase finally woke the twins, who added their cries to the cacophony.

Emma leant down into the playpen and scooped the babies up with some difficulty, one in each arm, and stood jigging them comfortingly and wondering what to do next. The terrier continued to tear around the garden and, on one circuit past the playpen, cocked its leg and marked one corner before shooting away again as Emma started towards it with a furious shout. Her cry distressed the twins again and the general noise level was so loud that it took a few minutes for Emma to realise that her neighbour was now out in the garden beyond the hedge, whistling and calling to the terrier.

Eventually, the terrier halted in its tracks, lifted an ear and then pelted down the lawn and disappeared through the hedge, leaving Barley standing stock still and looking bewildered.

"Yes, Milo, but you're a very bad dog," came a slightly quavery male voice from beyond the hedge in response to further yapping. "I'm very sorry," the voice called. "I hope he hasn't done any damage? He's burrowed right under the fence on this side and I'm afraid I hadn't noticed. I'll have to get the hole filled in."

"Thanks for calling him back," Emma replied. "There's no harm done," she added, not wanting to trouble an elderly gentleman with any details.

"That's good. I didn't realise you had a dog," said her invisible neighbour.

"I don't," Emma responded.

"We're just visiting," Theresa explained. "I've got a labrador."

"Splendid," the neighbour replied courteously. "I'll take Milo in now and I'll make sure the hole is dealt with before I let him out again."

"Thank you," Emma called and, as she turned to carry the twins indoors, she could hear her neighbour admonishing his pet in diminuendo.

"Well!" exclaimed Theresa, sounding rather thrilled at the whole episode as she moved to take hold of Barley's lead but, not wanting to discuss it with her, Emma continued on her way. Stepping into the kitchen, she found an atmosphere like a sauna and it took her only a moment to realise the cause. She had left the kettle to boil and it had plainly not switched itself off properly, as had happened on a few occasions in the past – although not lately. If the automatic switch had failed, it would have continued boiling until the room was full of steam.

She hurried through the fog and out into the sitting room, where she was able to lay the twins safely on a rug already spread out on the floor. Then she hastened back to the kitchen to assess the damage. She went immediately across to check the kettle and found that it had boiled completely dry. The cupboard fronts above it were running with condensation and the air was laden with moisture, so she threw open the kitchen windows.

Theresa, who was standing on the back doorstep with her dog, peering in, asked interestedly what had gone wrong, and Emma explained politely, whilst wishing that her unwelcome visitor would go away and leave her in peace to sort out the chaos.

She refilled the kettle but found that it would not switch on.

"The fuse has probably blown," Theresa pointed out unnecessarily. She stepped inside, bringing Barley with her, and headed over towards the sink, helping herself to a pretty china bowl off the draining rack, which she filled with water.

Emma had begun to wipe her cupboard fronts with a cloth but, as she saw Theresa bending down with the bowl, it dawned on her that she was intending to offer it to her dog.

"Don't use that!" she protested sharply. "Let me get you something else."

As Theresa grudgingly returned the bowl to the rack, Emma rummaged hastily in a cupboard and found an empty ice-cream tub, ran a good amount of cold water into it and placed it on the floor for Barley.

Theresa sat down at the table and watched her dog lapping from the tub, while Emma returned to her cleaning up.

"Now, how are we going to manage about that cup of tea?" her immovable guest asked chattily. "You could use a saucepan on the hob. That's what I do when there's a power cut."

Unable to think of any way of shifting Theresa until some tea had been supplied, Emma bowed to the inevitable and filled a jug with water, heating it in the microwave and then adding it to the teapot.

"Who is your neighbour with the little dog, dear?" Theresa asked, while Emma was thus occupied.

"I don't know?" she replied shortly. "I've never met him."

"It'll be a house in the next street – Wallace Road.

I suppose it'll have the same sort of numbering as this street, as they run parallel. What's the number of the house opposite you?"

"Twenty – but I think the houses along the back of us are older, so the numbering may be different."

"I'll go round on the way home and have a look."

Once she had handed Theresa a mug of tea, Emma went to fetch Millie and Joel. She fastened them into their bouncy chairs so that she could drink her tea and work out what to do next.

Theresa seemed to take an inordinate length of time to finish her drink, while Barley wandered round the kitchen unchecked and kept Emma on edge by sniffing at the babies and wagging her tail with an enthusiasm which threatened to do some damage.

When at last Theresa put her mug down, she said, "I'll just help you clean up the playpen, dear. Then I must be going."

"Don't worry," Emma said with more haste than gratitude. "I'll sort it later."

She had already made up her mind that the playpen would need dismantling and a thorough disinfecting.

"It's no trouble," Theresa returned. "It'll only take a mo and I can just use your sponge and a drop of soap."

She moved to help herself to the washing-up sponge as she spoke but was interrupted by the ringing of the doorbell.

"Don't!" Emma exclaimed in alarm. "I'd really rather you didn't start anything," she told Theresa over her shoulder, feeling extremely harassed, as she went to answer the summons from the front door.

To her complete surprise, she found Nick on the doorstep,

holding a cotton shopping bag and looking somewhat awkward. Emma could not hide her initial puzzlement at his presence. However, in the circumstances, she was almost pleased to see him and her expression changed swiftly from doubt to acceptance.

"Oh, Nick!" she exclaimed with unforced cordiality. "Do come in."

He in his turn looked startled and a little wary but, as she was already walking back to the kitchen, he followed her through the hallway.

"Theresa!" Emma announced brightly. "This is Nick, a friend who's come to help."

"Well, I just dropped round to bring -" he began, but encountering a glare from Emma, he broke off. After a moment, he put his bag on the table and said guardedly, "I'm happy to help, of course."

"So I won't keep you any longer," Emma told Theresa firmly. "I'm sure you'll be glad to get home. Thank you for the bananas."

CHAPTER 9

Having escorted Theresa and Barley inexorably out of the front door, Emma returned to the kitchen to face Nick's puzzlement.

"Oh," she sighed with relief. "I thought she'd never leave. I'm sorry I roped you into supporting my story," she added, shamefaced. "But I'm so pleased to have got rid of her."

"That's okay. I just dropped round with a helping of casserole from Charlie – it's in that bag." He nodded towards the table. "But I'm happy to help now I'm here."

"No need. I only said that to persuade Theresa to go," she replied, lifting a plastic box out of the bag as she spoke and peeping inside.

"It's beef casserole and very tasty," Nick said. "We had it for lunch and I can recommend it."

Enlightenment dawned. "Ah, you've had lunch with Ed and Charlie and little Dan. Where's Penny?"

"Penny?"

"I thought she was invited as well?"

"She *was*, but she's a nurse and she's doing a lot of weekend shifts at the moment, so she couldn't make it. We thought we'd do lunch again sometime, when her shifts change."

After an uncomfortable pause, he went on, "Charlie would have brought the casserole round herself but Dan took a bit of a tumble and hit his head, so they were patching him up and wondering whether to take him to the hospital for a check-up, and Charlie asked if I could drop it round to you. It's not far out of my way back to the main road."

"Is Dan alright?"

"I think he'll be fine, but I guess it's always best to be cautious with a blow to the head."

Joel began to grumble and Nick crouched down beside his chair and waved a toy for him.

"So who is Theresa? And why were you so keen to see the back of her?" he asked curiously.

"She goes to my church and I think she's genuinely trying to be kind – although I suspect that she's also lonely and looking for things to do. Anyway, her idea of what's helpful is nothing like mine and, whatever she does, I end up feeling bad. If I try to explain it to you, I'll sound really ungrateful – and sometimes I think I am."

"Explain anyway."

"Today, for example, she brought me some bananas for Millie and Joel and they're not even on solids yet." She picked up the old, plastic carrier bag as she spoke. "It sounds like an understandable mistake, but I *have* told her before. And then, I bet they'll be something she's bought cheaply because they're near their use-by date or something."

Looking inside the bag, she exclaimed in involuntary revulsion. "See! This is typical," she went on, and gingerly lifted out a bunch of dark brown, rather squashed and oozing bananas.

"Throw them away," Nick recommended cavalierly.

"I will," she replied, suiting the action to the words. "But that's what I often end up doing and it's such a waste."

"Maybe she has a phobia for throwing things away and wants you to do it for her," Nick suggested facetiously.

"Unfortunately, I think she just prefers to buy stuff as cheaply as possible - which is fine if it's usable, but not if I end up binning it. Maybe she has very different standards for what she's willing to eat - she frequently shocks me with her attitudes towards cleanliness and safety."

"Was it general distaste or something specific – other than the threat of black bananas – that had wound you up today?" Nick asked sympathetically.

So Emma recounted the chapter of accidents which she had endured that afternoon and, in the telling, she found that there was a funny side and laughed till her sides ached as she described the chaos caused by her neighbour's little dog and the kitchen full of steam.

Nick laughed with her and, when he had recovered his breath, offered to help with the clean-up operation.

Both babies were now rather fretful and Emma explained that they were hungry and that she ought to feed them before she did anything else. "I'll deal with the cleaning up later," she finished.

"That's okay," Nick replied. "You sort the twins out and I'll make a start with the rest. Just tell me where to find fuses and disinfectant and we'll take it from there."

"There's no need -," Emma began.

"If you won't tell me, I'll go and look for myself," Nick warned her cheerily.

"In that case," she submitted. She realised that she would be especially grateful for help with replacing the fuse for the kettle, as she had never attempted anything like that before. She supposed she would have to learn sometime, but perhaps she could be forgiven for not wanting to think about it now when there was so much else to cope with.

She showed Nick the cleaning equipment under the kitchen sink and the tool box in the cupboard under the stairs, which she thought must contain screwdrivers, fuses and the like. Then she took the twins away upstairs and left him to make a start.

As she sat quietly, first with Joel and then with Millie, Emma found herself wondering about Nick. He seemed so kind; but she had thought the same that summer six years ago when she had met him at Ed's birthday party. She remembered their first meeting so clearly: the instant attraction, the delight when he had indicated that he would like to see her again. Emma had been studying in Bristol at the time and had already found a job with a local firm for the long vacation, so they had spent the whole of that wonderful summer seeing each other as often they could contrive, travelling between Bristol and Portsmouth, where he was then working; phoning, talking, sharing as much of each other's lives as possible – or so she had believed, until she had received that cruel text message from him. She could still remember it word for word: 'Not coming over this w/e. Can't see you anymore. Sorry. Nick.' And she could still remember the utter devastation and incomprehension she had felt. But it was best not to think about that, best not to expend any more time or emotion on trying to understand what had gone wrong, what about him she had misunderstood so badly.

As soon as she could, she should go downstairs and

tell him to leave, she decided. But neither Joel nor Millie were in a hurry, and by the time they were both satisfied, her righteous indignation had faded again. She supposed that she must concede him some virtues, since he had been willing to stay and help.

She peeped out of the back bedroom window to see whether Nick was cleaning the playpen and found that he had apparently moved on and was now hard at work in the flowerbed she had begun weeding after lunch. As she watched, he mopped his brow, laid down the fork he had been wielding and pulled off his shirt, tossing it over the branch of an overhanging hazel tree, before picking up a spade and beginning to cut a neat edge to the lawn along the perimeter of the flowerbed.

Emma drew back and, in the awkwardness of the moment, elected to stay upstairs and change the twins' nappies before daring to venture anywhere near the back garden.

When she did go down, she laid the twins on their rug in the sitting room, where there was nothing on which they could possibly hurt themselves should they roll, and went back to the kitchen, calling towards the back door, "Would you like a drink?"

"I'd love a glass of water," came the cheerful reply.

Taking as much time as she could to fill a glass at the cold tap, find a plate and put a few biscuits out, and arrange everything on a small tray, she eventually risked stepping out into the garden. She walked slowly down the garden, keeping her eyes on her burden for as long as possible, but found that she need not have been so diffident as Nick had already shrugged himself back into his shirt and fastened a couple of the buttons.

"Thanks," he said, draining the glass. "It's thirsty work."

"I should be thanking *you*," Emma pointed out.

"I enjoy it. Penny only has a paved yard and a few tubs, so I miss out nowadays."

"How did you get on with the kettle?" Emma asked, changing the subject.

"It's working again. It was the fuse, as you said; but I would guess the automatic switch is unreliable, so perhaps buy yourself a new kettle?"

"I've been meaning to for weeks but not quite getting round to it. What about the playpen?"

"Well, I don't know whether my ideas of hygiene match up to your standards," he remarked quizzically. "I mopped up first with kitchen towel, which I have disposed of. I took everything apart, wiped all the pieces down with disinfectant, started again with a clean cloth and rinsed everything off, then dried it as well as I could with some more kitchen towel. Then I put it all back together and left the playpen out on the patio to air off - but I could carry it indoors if you prefer?"

"No, that's fine, thank you. You've been really helpful. Would you like a biscuit?"

"Best not. My hands are dirty," he twinkled.

"I must get back to the twins but I'll leave the plate on the kitchen table in case you want something to eat once you've washed your hands."

"I'd better be going soon," he remarked, glancing at his watch.

"Of course."

"There's lots of work out here."

"I know," she agreed ruefully. "It's hard to find the time to keep on top of it."

"I could –" he began hesitantly. "If it would help, I - perhaps I could drop round sometime and give you a hand?"

"What would Penny say?" Emma asked the first thing that came into her mind.

"Why would she say anything?"

"I don't know. I – er – I thought maybe she'd prefer you not to." Emma ground to a halt, her cheeks flushed, unable to think how to explain her doubts.

"I'll ask her," he said, sounding mystified.

Emma thought it highly unlikely that he would do anything of the kind. It was impossible to imagine that his current girlfriend could view with any complacency the prospect of his doing occasional gardening for a former girlfriend, however far in the past the relationship had been.

She thought it over during the course of the evening and concluded that he would definitely not call round again. His visit and his assistance had been the result of a combination of circumstances which were highly unlikely to recur. In retrospect, it troubled her on Penny's account that she had allowed Nick to stay and help but she could not quite think why, nor could she decide at first whether she could, in fact, have done anything to prevent him - until she recalled, with mortification, her behaviour on finding him on her doorstep. She had been led astray by her longing to disencumber herself of Theresa's burdensome presence and had invited him in with great friendliness when she should have simply taken delivery of the casserole and allowed him to go. She had been selfish, thoughtless and misleading;

she had hardly shown Christian charity to Theresa; she was ashamed of herself and petitioned the Lord for help to do better in future.

When she phoned Charlie to thank her for the delicious casserole, she was able to enquire after Dan and found that he was none the worse for his fall. Ed and Charlie had taken him to the hospital, because a blow to the temple might be dangerous, but a thorough medical examination had revealed no serious damage and, with that reassurance, they had accepted the information leaflet on head injuries proffered by the nurse, headed home and thought no more about it.

Emma was not so successful in avoiding thinking about her disrupted afternoon. It took much prayer to lift her out of the despondency which followed her moment of self-knowledge and for several days thereafter she was still conscious of a depression of the spirits, which afflicted her from time to time.

In this mood of dejection, she was very glad to hear from her brother, Luke, one evening a few days later. He called to let her know that he would be in the UK for some meetings the following week and that, as most of his commitments were in London, he wondered whether Emma would be willing to put him up.

"I can book a hotel if you prefer," he added. "Don't want to give you more work."

"Oh, Luke, it would be great to see you," she replied unreservedly, her spirits lifting at the thought. "Please do come and stay with me. I'd be so glad of some company."

"Thought you might."

"How long can you stay?"

"Fly in Monday afternoon; leave Friday morning."

"Wonderful! Will you want meals?"

"Breakfast definitely; a couple of evening meals, at least. May have other plans for one or two evenings. Can I let you know?"

"Of course. I can always get something out of the freezer, if your plans change. I'm so looking forward to it. I thought it might be ages before I'd see you again, as you were over here in May. That's only about six weeks ago. They don't normally let you come over that often, do they?"

"I haven't asked before - no reason," he said, sounding slightly cagey.

"There isn't a problem with work, is there?"

"No, nothing like that, Sis," he replied jauntily, leaving Emma to guess that his real reason for arranging another trip to the UK so soon was to support her.

CHAPTER 10

In preparation for Luke's arrival, Emma planned a couple of his favourite meals and went out and bought a new kettle.

Although he was busy on Monday evening and tied up with various business meetings throughout the day on Tuesday and Thursday, Luke had kept the whole of Wednesday free to spend time with his sister and his nephew and niece. The weather was glorious and they decided to venture out for the day, taking a picnic for the adults and lots of equipment and amusements for the twins. It was enormous fun and Emma felt quite light-hearted with sun and congenial company as they headed home at the end of a long day.

Luke had offered to drive and she had let him, as she knew he preferred to have both occupation and control. Millie and Joel slumbered peacefully in the back of the car after so much fresh air, novelty and stimulation.

Thinking of his casually good-humoured interaction with Millie and Joel throughout the day and the hilarity he had provoked again at bath time the previous evening, she remarked drowsily that he ought to get married and have children of his own.

"I'm beginning to think so," he replied. "I'm out again tomorrow night," he added as an apparent non sequitur.

"Oh? Is it a business dinner?"

"You could call it that," he responded and, glancing idly at him, Emma saw a slight flush along his cheekbones."

Now she was wide awake.

"I never asked you where you went on Monday night," she said mischievously. "Was that another 'business' dinner?"

"Might've been," he replied with mock haughtiness.

"Is she pretty?"

"Very."

"How long have you known her?"

"Seven weeks."

"Well, I shan't interrogate you any further right now, but I expect to hear all about her soon."

"Mmm. Just don't tell Mum."

"Of course not. She rang at the weekend and I didn't even mention that you were coming over. She was more interested in telling me about an outbreak of some fever that they've been dealing with. That's because, when she asked after the twins, I made the mistake of commenting that Millie had seemed a bit off-colour one day last week. I should've known that would lead to a dissertation on the many greater challenges which the Nepalese face daily."

Luke grinned at her acerbity, but Emma immediately regretted her pointed remark.

"I made a vow recently to be more patient with people's foibles," she owned. "But I keep failing."

"Don't we all."

"But shouldn't we be able to see some improvement? If we really want to change and we pray about it, surely we should expect to see at least gradual progress?"

"I rarely catch God at work in that sort of situation,"

Luke replied. "Only when I look back a while later do I think I see growth."

"Perhaps I'm too impatient. It would be nice if there were a quick fix."

"What brought on this soul searching?"

"Theresa Halton."

"Who's she?"

"D'you remember the lady who was babysitting during Sam's service and gave Joel her keys to suck?"

"I remember that you were upset. Is that what she did?"

"That and other things. She keeps calling round – and she irritates me every time in some way or other. It reached the point where I realised that I was becoming quite uncharitable."

"Can't imagine that."

"It's true – at least, my thoughts were often mean-spirited – and I was ashamed. So I resolved to try to be more tolerant, but progress is slow to the point of being indiscernible."

"What are you trying to achieve?" Luke asked, sounding interested rather than critical.

"What do you mean?"

"Are you hoping for more patience when she annoys you or to learn to find her behaviour less annoying in the first place?"

"I think, the former. I can't imagine ever finding her peculiarities less annoying."

"Unless you can change your perception of her? Understand why she behaves that way? Not that I'm any example to follow," Luke admitted. "I should try harder to be get along with Rachel, for a start."

"Do you suppose she ever prays these days?"

"Rachel?"

"Yes."

"No idea."

"I often think I really ought to talk to her sometime about faith. She used to seem so committed."

"She chose to marry a non-Christian: it's often difficult after that."

"I suppose – but it's Harry's worldly ambition and his materialism that particularly seem to have led her away from God. She makes me think of the seed that fell among thorns – where faith is choked by life's worries, riches and pleasures."

"Keep praying," Luke recommended.

"Do you?"

"Much more than I used to."

"Would *you* marry a non-Christian?"

"No. What kind of marriage would it be, where you don't share the one thing that should be most important to you?"

Clearly, despite their mother's concern, Luke regarded himself as a Christian. Emma hoped she could also deduce from this conversation that he was dating a Christian girl, but she respected his reserve and did not press for more information.

She enjoyed the rest of her brother's stay and secretly wished she could look forward to another visit from him in the not too distant future, but was quite confounded when, as he was about to depart, he remarked that he hoped to be back again in about six weeks' time.

"Are you serious?" she asked, doubtfully.

"The tap's still dripping in your bathroom. I'll be back to check whether you've had it fixed!"

"In that case, I'll never get it fixed and you'll have to keep coming back to check up on me."

"Joking aside, would you be happy to put me up, if I can arrange another trip?"

"You're always welcome – you know that."

"Thanks, Sis."

Reflecting later on the various conversations she had had with her brother, Emma rapidly jettisoned the notion that he was planning a further visit to England simply to support her. That her situation might be an added inducement she did not doubt, but she felt certain that there must be another motive.

He had denied that there was any problem at work so she began to suspect that he was seriously attracted to this girl he had mentioned and was taking steps to pursue the association.

If that were the case, she feared for the outcome of a relationship conducted at such a distance. It was one thing to maintain an already established connection with half a world between them, although that would be challenging enough, but to build and nurture a fledgling romance with all the constraints imposed by a vast geographical separation, must be almost impossible, and must render them vulnerable to every kind of heartache and misunderstanding.

She prayed frequently for her brother and especially for his Christian walk and for his happiness and, in doing so, was reminded to pray for her sister as well. She began to include Rachel and her husband and children regularly in her prayers, asking God to watch over them both physically and spiritually and draw them to Him as Saviour and Lord.

When her sister rang one evening as Emma was sorting through some dry washing for ironing, her first instinct was to wonder what Rachel wanted but, as they ran through the requisite civil enquiries about their respective families and a discussion of the vagaries of the British weather, Emma chided herself for her cynicism. By roundabout ways, Rachel introduced the topic of holidays and finally broached what seemed to be the real reason for her call, saying that she had been wondering whether she and the children might pay Emma a visit in August on their way to Gatwick.

"We have a flight out to Florida booked for Tuesday evening – the ninth of August – and now Harry has got a meeting in London that afternoon which he can't miss, so I wondered whether I could bring the kids down earlier in the day and spend a bit of time with you and the twins. Then Harry could meet us at yours and we could head off for our flight. I've hardly seen you since – since Sam died and I thought maybe you'd be glad of some company."

"You'd be very welcome," Emma replied, a little surprised at the expression of sisterly concern. "Do your children know about Sam now?"

"Yes, one of Tilly's friends had an elderly dog that sadly had to be put down, so I had to explain about death to them all. I mentioned Sam at the same time, which worked very well, because they were more focussed on Rosie – the dog – and didn't ask lots of questions."

Emma could think of nothing to say.

"If it's alright with you," Rachel continued, "we'll turn up during the afternoon on the ninth and then we can have a quick meal with you once Harry arrives and then drive on to Gatwick."

"That's fine. Would you like to make more of a day of it and come for lunch as well?"

"We can't get to you that early," Rachel warned. "Tilly has a pool party that morning, which I don't want her to miss. It's for the daughter of one of the top London barristers, who just happens to live locally. They're fantastically wealthy and they have this amazing house. The party will be in their own grounds and there'll be an entertainer and caterers to provide the lunch and everything. It's the kind of opportunity that only comes along occasionally. While she's at the party, I'll be frantically getting everything packed for the three weeks away. It takes so much planning to get the family organised with all the things they might want for that kind of trip."

Emma could see several flaws in her sister's position but she kept them to herself.

"What would the children like for tea?" she asked mildly.

"Maybe pasta or pizza," Rachel suggested. "But could you avoid any cooked cheese or cheese sauce, as Clemmie just won't eat it. Jago isn't keen on anything spicy or any salad and Tilly doesn't like ham or beef. Also, none of them like mushroom, melon, pineapple or blueberries, and Clemmie can't have grapes."

"Goodness, there's not much left, is there?"

"Tell me about it! It's a nightmare! That's why I said to Harry that it would be a disaster to try and meet him at Gatwick for a meal before we check in. Eating out is virtually impossible when they're so choosy. Of course, they'd eat chips and chicken dippers like a shot, but I try to avoid giving them fried food. I don't want the girls to put on weight as they get older. It would be so disappointing if they turned into the kind of chubby teenagers that everyone pities. I always remember your school friend, Charlotte. Such a shame she was overweight. None of the boys ever looked at her twice."

"But now she is very happily married and has a lovely little boy."

"And since her husband is no lightweight, presumably their 'lovely little boy' will turn into another fat adult."

"They're not *fat* – just a little solid, perhaps. Besides, looks aren't nearly as important as character; and Ed and Charlie are two of the nicest people I know," Emma said defensively.

When she came off the phone, conscious as always of some exasperation with her sister, Emma reflected that her cynicism had been proved justified. Apparently, she was considered a better option for providing a healthy meal for three fussy children than the restaurants at Gatwick might be. Had that not been the case, she had no doubt that her sister would never have come up with the notion of paying her a visit.

Emma returned to folding the washing. As she gently smoothed and piled the twins' little vests, she pondered on her difficult relationship with her sister and it occurred to her that this projected visit might be an opportunity to build bridges or mend fences. She prayed that the Lord might be able to use it in some way in accordance with his will – 'his good, pleasing and perfect will'.

CHAPTER 11

Waking early on Saturday morning, Emma peeped out of the curtains and, seeing the unbroken cerulean blue of the summer sky, decided that she would use whatever time she could find during the day to tackle some of the outstanding tasks in the garden.

Filled with unaccustomed energy and enthusiasm, she had showered, dressed, read her Bible and breakfasted before the twins had stirred. She set the playpen up in the garden and went to find the equipment she would need, before checking on Millie and Joel. By then it was half past seven in the morning and the twins were awake, lying in their cots and playing happily with their feet. Feeding and dressing them was never a speedy business, but Emma enjoyed it so she did not hurry them.

Millie and Joel were both in a sunny humour that matched the day outside and they laughed as Emma applied sun-cream to their sweet faces and delightfully rounded limbs. They were not so keen on the fitting of sun hats but were happy enough to be carried outside and propped up in the playpen with various cushions and pillows. They were almost capable of sitting unaided, but Emma still liked to give them plenty of support and padding. She put various toys within reach and made a start on weeding the flowerbed nearest to the playpen so that she could keep an easy eye on them.

She had not been at work for very long and she was enjoying the warm sun on her back, the smell of the disturbed earth and the sense of progress, when she heard the distant ring of the doorbell. She got to her feet reluctantly, hoping it would not be Theresa or some other unwanted visitor.

Opening the front door rather cautiously and peering round, she found Nick standing there. Having made up her mind that he would not call round again, she was astonished to see him on her doorstep. He grinned in amusement at the wariness with which she stole a look at him through the gap of the barely opened door.

"Good morning," he said jauntily. "I've got a free day so I've come over to see if you'd like some more help with the garden."

"That's very kind of you," she replied, gathering her wits and opening the door wider.

"I've brought some kit," he said. "I'll fetch it from the car"

He was back in a few minutes with a collection of tools, and Emma saw that he was dressed very casually, ready for heavy work on a hot day.

"Where do you want me to start?" he asked.

"Actually, I'd just begun weeding out the back," Emma replied. "Do you want to come through?"

"Sure."

He followed her through the house and out into the back garden.

"That's a good set up," he approved when he saw Millie and Joel in their playpen.

"It usually keeps them happy for a little while at least," Emma agreed.

"If you carry on where you've started and I tackle the flowerbed at the foot of the garden, then we can work towards one another and hopefully meet in the middle," Nick suggested, having surveyed the terrain.

They worked for quite a long time in a silence broken only by occasional questions from Nick as to Emma's opinion of self-sown alkanet, purple toadflax and the like, but her mind was turning over and over her puzzlement as to his presence in her garden, and eventually she asked, "How's Penny?"

"Very well," he replied cheerily. "She sends her regards. Have you had any more visits from the dogs of your acquaintance?"

"No, none."

"The playpen seems to have survived."

"Yes. Thank you."

They relapsed into silence, but Emma was very much aware of his presence in her garden and of the sounds of his fork and trowel being briskly wielded, which formed a counterpoint to the continuous hum of busy insects on the nearby flowers.

When the twins got bored of confinement, Emma cleaned off her hands, spread a rug out on the lawn, lifted Millie and Joel out of the playpen and let them roll on the rug and play with their own hands and feet for a while. However, that required supervision, so she had to abandon her weeding. Nick carried on working, but even resting on the rug with the twins, Emma was conscious of the ever-increasing heat of the day and she began to feel guilty at his continued exertions.

"If you could keep an eye on the twins, I'll fetch some drinks," she suggested.

"That'd be great, but I ought to wash my hands first."

He disappeared indoors and reappeared a little later with a tray and two glasses of water, which he brought down to Emma.

"I thought, since I was in the kitchen anyway, I might as well fetch the drinks," he remarked, sitting down on the grass next to the rug and taking a long draught from one of the glasses. "You've got a nice place here," he commented, looking round the garden. "Ed tells me you don't have a mortgage."

"Yes. Sam was able to buy it outright."

"He was a lucky man," Nick said with feeling. "It must be a relief to you to know that you won't have to move out anytime soon," he added.

"Yes."

"How are you getting on now - er - generally?" he asked rather awkwardly.

"Not so bad, I suppose," Emma replied. "The twins are getting easier – they amuse themselves for a bit longer and they sleep through the night better. They'll be six months old in – goodness! – in less than three weeks."

"Did you enjoy having your brother to stay?"

"Yes, it was great, thanks," she replied automatically, slightly surprised that he knew of Luke's visit but assuming that she must have mentioned it at some point or that he had heard it from Ed. "It would be nicer if he weren't so far away."

"Do you think he'll want to move back to the UK sometime?"

"I've no idea. Maybe. It probably depends on the incentive."

At this point, Joel rolled towards Nick and gurgled, and Nick picked him up quite naturally and sat him on his knee, bouncing him up and down and talking to him.

Emma watched for a while, enjoying Joel's pleasure, set against the backdrop of the colourful summer garden, with the occasional dance of a passing yellow brimstone or tortoiseshell butterfly and surrounded by the sweet scent of sun-warmed grass; but when Nick's gaze lifted to hers, she looked hastily away and, for the sake of something to do, lifted Millie on to her own lap.

She played rather self-consciously with her daughter, aware that Nick's eyes were still on her, but eventually he lay back on the grass and lifted Joel over his head, to the accompaniment of much merriment. After a few minutes of this, he swung Joel back down on to the rug, stood up and said that he had better get back to work, walking away briskly.

Emma sat for a little longer, playing with the twins rather absent-mindedly and trying not to think about Nick; trying not to remember that idyllic summer six years ago when she had been so rapturously happy, so sure that they would be together for ever.

The twins went rather more reluctantly back into the playpen the second time. They both grumbled for a time, dozed for perhaps half an hour and then woke and complained rather more vociferously, so that Emma's weeding was again curtailed. She wondered whether the temperature was rather too much for them and told Nick that she thought she had better take them indoors.

"I'm sorry to leave you to it. Do stop whenever you've had enough," she said.

"Don't mind me," he replied, sounding completely sanguine. "I was expecting to get on by myself."

Feeling as though she had been dismissed, Emma retreated to the shade of the house and amused the twins as best she could, whilst wondering why Nick had come, what he was doing and how long he meant to stay.

Having fed and changed the twins shortly after noon, Emma began to ponder the conundrum of lunch for herself and Nick. Should she provide some food, she wondered, or was he planning to leave shortly? Perhaps he had brought his own food. Her doubts were partially answered by the sound of a motor starting up and, looking out, she saw that Nick had cleared the lawn and fetched the mower from the shed and was just beginning to cut the grass. Plainly, he was not about to depart.

She put Millie and Joel in their bouncy chairs and speedily began to lay the kitchen table with crusty bread and butter, olives, cheese, salad and a bowl of fruit. The twins, who were in a rather better humour now their stomachs were full, kicked and blew bubbles and watched her moving around the kitchen. She added cutlery, crockery, glasses and a jug of apple juice and, satisfied with her handiwork, went back to entertaining the twins while she waited for the hum of the mower to cease.

When silence finally descended on the back garden, Emma went outside rather shyly "It looks very neat," she said, seeing the straight lines up and down her lawn. Her own attempt several weeks ago had been much more random.

"The hedge and some of the shrubs could do with trimming," he said. "And there's still quite a lot more weeding to do, but I thought I'd get on with cutting the lawn, while you weren't wanting to use it."

She thanked him and invited him to join her indoors for lunch.

Nick said grace before they ate and then tucked in with a hearty appetite. Conversation was a little strained over the meal. Emma asked politely about Nick's work and they also discussed Charlie, Ed and Dan and agreed what fantastic people they were, but it was almost a relief when the twins began to get grumpy and to require attention. The two adults ended up with a twin apiece and spent the rest of the meal, jigging them on their laps or walking them round the room, while grabbing the occasional bite to eat, and there was little opportunity for intelligent dialogue.

At the end of the meal, Emma took the twins away and put them down in their cots for a nap. By the time she returned to the kitchen, Nick had cleared the table and stacked the dishwasher and was just on his way back out into the garden.

"Will they sleep for long?" he asked.

"A bit short of an hour, maybe."

"I don't know how you get anything much done," he remarked.

"I don't really."

"You're doing incredibly well."

Emma was embarrassed at the warmth of his tone and said hastily that she had had a considerable amount of help.

"Quite right too," he said firmly. "You deserve a great deal of help in the – the circumstances."

"Is that why *you're* here?"

"I think you know why I'm here," he replied curtly and disappeared out of the back door.

Emma wondered what he meant. Did he feel sorry for her? Was he trying to make amends for his former treatment of her? She could not understand him - but she supposed drearily that she had never understood him.

She felt distinctly uncomfortable about joining him in the back garden so she set up her ironing board in the kitchen and did some long overdue pressing of blouses, pillowcases and the like. It was hot work for a sunny day in mid-July and, by the time the twins were beginning to stir again, she was thinking longingly of a cool drink of water. She realised that Nick must be even hotter so, leaving the twins to complain in their cots for a little longer, she filled a glass and took it out to him.

"Thanks very much," he said, and gulped it down thirstily. "I'd better be going soon," he added, checking his watch, as he had on his previous visit.

"You've made great progress," she replied gratefully, looking round at the tidy flowerbeds and smooth lawn. "It really is kind of you to give up your Saturday like this."

She took the glass from him without meeting his gaze and withdrew to the house, occupying herself with the twins until he came indoors.

"I've spent all my time in the garden today," he said as he was preparing to depart. "But are there any other jobs around the house that I could help with?"

"No, I don't think so. Oh, are you any good at

mending taps?" she added before she had thought about the inadvisability of involving him any further.

"It depends what's wrong with the tap. Shall I have look?"

"Oh, don't worry."

"I can easily take a quick look."

"Well, it's the bath tap upstairs," Emma admitted reluctantly.

Nick headed up the stairs two at a time and came down a few minutes later commenting that she probably needed a new washer. "I can't sort that now, I'm afraid. Can it wait?"

"Oh yes," she said quickly. "It's been dripping for months. Don't worry about it."

"Okay. See you then. God bless."

He was gone before she could thank him properly.

CHAPTER 12

That evening, once the twins were asleep, Emma allowed herself to think about Nick, to consider all that she knew about him and all that she remembered.

He had been twenty-four when they had first met and she had been twenty, which meant he was perhaps about thirty now. In fact, she recalled very clearly that his birthday was on the first of June, less than a month after Ed's, so he was definitely thirty.

To her eyes six years ago, he had been the most attractive man she had ever seen, and when she had realised that the attraction was mutual, she had been overjoyed. In her memory, the sun had shone for the whole of that happy summer. That was impossible, of course. They had met on the fifth of May and he had ended their relationship on the twenty-first of August and this was England – it must have rained at some point during those three and a half blissful months.

The closer she had grown to Nick over those months, the more she had discovered his many strengths – his humour, his kindness, his intelligence, his integrity (so she had thought) – and the more she had loved him. And she had believed that he had felt the same. He had certainly told her so on a number of occasions. She had been completely certain that their future lay together, stretching on into old age, and she had regarded herself as fully committed to him – engaged in every way, save for the formality of a ring. That he had felt equally committed she had been totally convinced. They had spoken many times of their future and their plans.

He had studied mathematics at Southampton University, which was where he and Ed had become friends, but when Emma met him he had already been working for two years in Portsmouth. He had seemed so grown up, so wise but such fun. Like Ed he had been heavily involved in his university Christian Union and had gone on to take on a number of roles in his local church. He had always said that he wanted to work for a few years in the secular world and then test his vocation for the ministry. And she - silly, adoring, devoted little Emma - had drunk it all in and thought he was the most dedicated, faultless young man she could ever hope to meet. She had hero-worshipped him. Perhaps he had found it too much to live up to; after all, no one could really be that perfect all the time.

In the relatively short time they had been together, Nick had never taken Emma to meet his parents. As his family had lived somewhere up on the border with Scotland, that had not seemed unreasonable and, of course, he had never met her parents either, since they were away in Nepal by then. Afterwards, Emma had wondered whether she should have seen it as a forewarning – as an indication of a lack of commitment on his part, but that summer, blind with happiness, she had simply been content to take each weekend with Nick as a gift and had given no real consideration to wider concerns. She knew he came from a large family with numerous siblings and half-siblings, his father having married Nick's mother some years after the death of his first wife. Nick had spoken of them all with affection and Emma had assumed that, in their contented lifetime together, she would eventually get to know and love each member of his family for herself, but there did not seem to be any hurry. When he had rejected her so offhandedly, all her assumptions about the future had come crashing down.

Some of Nick's virtues were certainly genuine, Emma mused. He really had been immensely kind. She could recall many examples of his willingness to help her and others, his patience and his prayerfulness. She had watched him again and again quietly serving without seeking notice or thanks. He had been kind then and, if she was honest, he was kind now. He had been concerned and compassionate on the day she had gone to see Charlie in the rain and found him there so unexpectedly, despite her own lack of courtesy towards him. He had been kind and considerate since then.

He was so good with the twins too. He seemed to have a natural ability to relate to babies and children unaffectedly. She remembered that he had joined her a couple of times when she had been helping with the crèche at her student church in Bristol and he had been a great asset: willing to pace the floor with a grizzling baby, play trains with a boisterous toddler, sing songs, read stories or even change nappies.

The best word to describe him was 'servant-hearted', she decided. But how was it that someone so unpretentiously good could have treated her so badly? Recalling those far-off, halcyon days of romantic infatuation, before he had broken her heart, Emma thought that her blind adoration had been excusable. He really had seemed entirely admirable. No wonder she had been so completely shocked by his sudden defection and by the cruel manner of it.

All through that summer, she had imagined that he loved her as much she loved him, but she must have been mistaken. He could not have walked away without a backward glance as he had done, if he had cared at all. And she had reacted to his desertion like an idiot, with hysterical tears (which he had fortunately never seen) and with repeated pleas that he might at least tell her what she had done wrong. "I don't understand," she had replied to his original text; and then later: "Please call me." She had left a number of answerphone messages too, until she had drearily acknowledged that there was not going to be any reply, any explanation, any hope of a reconciliation, and had decided she should not abase herself any further.

Now she could not avoid the realisation that his actions then had been entirely out of keeping with his character. She had not previously seen that so clearly. At the time, she had been too preoccupied with searching her memory and her conscience for any fault of her own, and later she had converted her grief into anger and had dwelt on the unpardonable cruelty of his behaviour. But what could possibly explain the anomaly of his astonishing heartlessness? Wild theories occurred to her only to be discarded. Did he suffer from some kind of split personality? There was no other evidence to suggest such a thing. Had he committed some crime and been fearful of discovery? The integrity of the rest of his behaviour made it unlikely. Might he have panicked at the speed with which their relationship had developed and acted in involuntary alarm? There was nothing to indicate any instability of character that might cause such an over-reaction.

It was as much a puzzle to Emma now as it had been six years ago, and although she turned it all round and round in her head for a long time, she reached no new conclusions.

During the intervening years, she had never heard Charlie or Ed mention that Nick was seeing any other girls, until Penny had so recently appeared on the scene, but perhaps he had had many girlfriends in that time and the subject had simply not come up or Ed had not even been aware of them. They had occasionally referred to Nick in passing when speaking of former friends and past times, and Emma had always been conscious of a pang of the old pain and had steered as quickly as possible away from the subject. She wondered now why she thought that Nick had not been with Penny for very long. True, they had only recently moved in together and Ed had remarked that it would be good to get to know her better, but now Emma came to think of it Penny had made some comment at Sam's service about being pleased to meet her 'at last', which suggested a rather longer acquaintance with Nick. Ed's remark was probably only a reflection of the fact that he had not seen much of Nick in recent years and, by corollary, did not know Penny very well.

And what – *what!* – did Penny think of Emma? What had Nick told her about that summer six years ago? Emma had once admitted to Sam, before they were married, that she had had a previous boyfriend, more than three years earlier. He had expressed humorous surprise that she had not received more interest since then but she had not explained that she had been too much attached to Nick and too hurt by his desertion to go out with others lightly. Once Sam had established that she had not slept with Nick, he had not wanted to hear anything more about him. But Penny's comment seemed to indicate that Nick had told her rather more about his former relationship than Emma had told Sam. As theirs had been an innocent association, in a sense he need not have said anything at all, but it was plain that he had spoken of it and of Emma. She blushed at the thought.

Perhaps more importantly, Emma wondered again what he had told Penny now about the hours he had spent helping Emma and the twins. Had he even mentioned it to her? He had said that he would ask Penny for her opinion but the mind boggled at how he would present that question. He had probably concluded that, with Penny out at work, he need proffer no account of how he had used his day.

Emma's thoughts moved on. Why had he come back today? Although he had previously offered his help, she had been certain that, in all the circumstances, he would not reappear; and yet he had turned up thoroughly equipped for a day's work and had stayed and toiled for many, many hours. Why? Was he, as she had wondered earlier, trying to atone in some way for his former behaviour? Did he pity her? Did he genuinely miss opportunities to do some proper gardening, as he had suggested? None of these explanations quite rang true. They each seemed an insufficient reason to justify the time he was sacrificing and the effort he had devoted to the task. But maybe all three reasons together might provide a sufficient incentive?

She wondered whether he would come back to fix the dripping tap. She wished now that she had not mentioned it. It must look as though she were asking for his help, wanting him to pay another visit. She almost squirmed with embarrassment at the idea. And she still felt very uneasy on Penny's account. Not because there was anything inappropriate in Nick's manner or anything to which Penny could take objection in his behaviour, save for the fact that he was spending so many hours at the house of another woman, however innocently, and that woman had once been his girlfriend, even if she was now a pitiable widow with two small children. Emma knew that, had their roles been reversed – had she been in Penny's shoes – she would have been unable to view his visits with any complacency.

As she always did eventually when uneasy and distressed, Emma turned to prayer. She took all her anxieties to the Lord and laid them out before Him, begging for wisdom, for clarity and for comfort. She felt a great deal better for having done so, although there was no immediate answer to her prayers. A peace seemed to still her restless thoughts and, once she got herself to bed, she slept soundly, waking refreshed and cheerful when the twins demanded attention at five in the morning.

CHAPTER 13

Emma's Bible passage later that morning was from John's Gospel – chapter fourteen. As she read, verse eighteen stirred an elusive memory: 'I will not leave you as orphans; I will come to you.' The section was Trinitarian and recounted Jesus' promises to his disciples to be with them even after his death and to send them the Holy Spirit after his resurrection. At first, she could not think where she might have heard the verse recently but then she remembered that the first part of the verse had come to mind just a few days after Sam's death and she had wondered whether it was intended as a reassuring message, a word of comfort.

Looking back over the past three months, she felt that she could genuinely see God's hand at work in the many instances of kindness and support she had received. He had not left her on her own but had sent her the company of friends and family. Charlie had been especially encouraging and sympathetic on many occasions, but Luke's stay had also been a real blessing and she had another such visit to look forward to. Her church family had rallied round and she had made a number of new friends at the toddler group and the Bible study meetings she attended. From her recent experiences, she had learnt lessons about trusting God and trusting in his sovereign goodness and compassion.

He really had not left her or the twins 'as orphans': what a good God he was!

She shared her thoughts with Charlie and Janet at church after the service that morning, and Janet smiled joyously and agreed that God was wonderfully good. "And you know what the consequence of that is, don't you?" she added. "You're in a perfect position to tell others about God's goodness or to offer comfort: 'we can comfort those in any trouble with the comfort we ourselves have received from God.' It's a great privilege to be an ambassador for Christ and you've been given a special gift to enable you to reach out to people who are struggling."

Charlie waited until Janet had moved away and then whispered to her friend that she thought Emma might be allowed a little more time first to find her feet.

"Perhaps Janet was encouraging me to think about it now," Emma said, "so that, if an opportunity arises later, I'm not taken by surprise and left with nothing to say."

"Yes, I suppose you never know when you're going to meet someone who needs to hear that God is good even in very tough times," Charlie agreed. "But I still think it's early days and you've got a lot to cope with, looking after two babies."

"It's not too bad," Emma replied.

"Well, I'm glad to hear you say that, because I think I may be expecting again and, if I'm right, I'll have two on my hands by next spring," Charlie confided.

Ed joined them with little Dan just as Emma was expressing her delight at the news.

He smiled comfortably and put an affectionate arm

round his wife's plump shoulders. "We're trying to catch up with you," he told Emma. "But we're doing it in easy stages."

"Easy!" exclaimed Charlie, teasing him. "You wouldn't say that if *you'd* got morning sickness!"

"True. Let's get you home. You'll need a snack and a rest soon."

Emma returned home with the twins, feeling positive. She wondered about Janet's words and passed her acquaintance under review to see whether she could think of anyone who was struggling and might need comfort, but she drew a blank, although it did occur to her that her sister was plainly trying to shut God out of her life and that perhaps Emma could help her to see that she needed to open the door and trust his goodness again.

Rachel's visit began to seem like a real opportunity to share something of her recent experiences of God's compassion and comfort, and she began to plan ways to introduce the topic. She thought of asking what Rachel had thought of Sam's service or whether she ever went to church these days or ever spoke to her children about Jesus or read the Bible with them. She thought of remarking casually that her faith had helped her a great deal in recent months or of mentioning that Luke's faith seemed to have grown. She ran various conversations round in her head but arrived at no definite plan. In the end, she concluded that it might be better to follow the Spirit's prompting and she simply prayed for the right opening.

She also remembered other family and friends regularly in her prayers, particularly Charlotte and Ed, and she began to petition the Lord for a safe and healthy pregnancy for

Charlie. However, her next contact with her friend brought bad news – not about the baby but about Ed's job.

When Charlie rang on Friday, Emma initially assumed that Charlie was going to suggest meeting up as they often did, but instead she found herself listening to a rather incoherent account of the politics of the company for which Ed worked, the threat of an anticipated merger and the likely consequences, what Ed's boss had said and how his colleagues had reacted. Emma could not follow all the details but she gathered that Ed and many of his peers had been put on notice that there was a likelihood of a considerable number or redundancies in the coming months.

"The timing couldn't be worse," Charlie went on, sounding uncharacteristically panic-stricken. "Here we are with another baby on the way and all the expense that involves, and Ed will be out of work. I don't know how we'll manage."

"It may not be as bad as that," Emma said reassuringly. "They may not have to make as many redundancies as they fear and, even if they do, it may not include Ed."

"But if it does, it will be a disaster! How could we pay our mortgage, let alone all the other outgoings? It's not as though *I* can start looking for a job just now."

"Ed would soon find another job, I'm sure," Emma encouraged her. "With his accountancy training, he's very employable."

"The job market isn't good at the moment," Charlie responded, refusing to be comforted.

"Let's pray about it," Emma suggested, knowing that she had found it enormously helpful when people had prayed for her in recent months.

Charlie did not demur so there and then Emma prayed for her friend at the other end of the phone line.

At the conclusion, Charlie thanked her, sounding rather less agitated. "I'm sorry to unload it all on you," she added, "but I didn't like to say anything to Ed. He's taking it fairly calmly – as always – but it won't help if he knows I'm in a state."

"No problem," Emma replied. "You've listened to plenty of *my* troubles. So is Ed looking round for other jobs?"

"He only heard about all this at work yesterday." Charlie's voice betrayed increasing stress again.

"Don't forget, God's already got a good plan," Emma reminded her friend quickly.

"I know," Charlie conceded. "I *do* know. It's just that this all came completely out of the blue and I feel so lousy, I just needed to scream."

"Scream away."

"It's okay. I feel a bit better already. But I hate the uncertainty of it, with the whole situation hanging over us, maybe for months. I think Ed will start looking at other openings as soon as possible and we agreed this morning that we'd have to trust God with all this. In fact, we were saying that you've been such a great example to us recently, still trusting God even when things are really difficult, but then Ed went off to work and I was thinking how steady and wise he'd been and how hard it must be for him – and his colleagues – to go into the office and do a day's work in an atmosphere of dread and perhaps even rivalry, and I got myself upset. It's silly because, as you said on Sunday, God is always good."

"That doesn't mean it's always easy," Emma admitted.

"But it does help if we keep holding on to that truth." She went on to recommend a few passages of scripture, which she had found encouraging in recent months and, once she had put the receiver down on a rather more cheerful friend, she smiled to herself at God's timing. On Sunday, Janet had encouraged her to share her experiences of God's goodness and comfort and, less than a week later, she had already been given an opportunity to do just that.

She returned to the task she had started a few minutes before Charlie's phone call and went on unpacking and setting up the steriliser that she had been given before the twins were born. As they would be six months old in less than a fortnight, she had decided it was time to begin preparing for the process of gradually weaning them on to formula milk and then on to solids.

Once she had set up the steriliser, she sat down to master the instructions but was again interrupted, this time by the doorbell. She wished she could ignore it but, as she hesitated, the bell was pressed again forcefully and she went reluctantly to answer its summons.

Theresa Halton stood squarely on the doorstep, her dog's lead in one hand and the usual, ominous, plastic bag in the other.

"Oh," said Emma, unwillingly remembering her resolve. "Would you like to come in?"

"Just for a minute, dear," Theresa replied, stepping purposefully inside. "I've brought you some cherry jam. My next-door neighbour made a batch a couple of days ago. She's got a glut of cherries so she gave me half a dozen jars and I thought of you."

She extracted a rather sticky jar from her bag as she spoke and handed it over.

"That's very kind," Emma said, with slightly strained civility. "Would you like a cup of tea?"

"I won't stop – although I'll just take a peep at the babies. I'm on my way round to see your neighbour. I think he'll be glad of some jam too."

"My neighbour?"

"Yes – Fred – at number thirty-two."

Emma looked blank.

"You know – Wallace Road – with Milo, the little terrier."

"Oh, I see," Emma said, beginning to understand.

"After his dog caused all that mischief, I called round to introduce myself and to check that he would get the hole mended – which he has, by the way. His son helped him. I discovered that he lives on his own – apart from Milo – and doesn't get out all that much. His wife died nearly ten years ago so we've got a lot in common – I lost my husband five years ago, you know. Anyway, he's not much good at cooking so I've been dropping round with meals for him. Barley and Milo are firm friends now."

Emma thought it was a delightful development for all sorts of reasons. She took Theresa into the kitchen, where the twins were playing happily in the playpen.

"My, they've grown," Theresa commented. "I haven't been round for a while because I've been rather busy keeping an eye on Fred. We've taken the dogs out for a few walks together too, which I'm sure is good for him, although he never goes far and, between you and me, dear, I think he's getting frailer by the day."

"I'm sorry he's not in very good health," Emma said. "Don't worry about us," she added, only too pleased to be spared frequent visits from Theresa. "We're managing perfectly well now, so do feel free to look after Fred instead."

"One thing I feel I should mention while I'm here," Theresa said, fiddling with her steel grey curls and sounding unusually stiff. "That young man who called last time I was here –." She paused.

"Nick?"

"You really must discourage him. It doesn't look at all appropriate for a personable young man like that to be calling on someone in your position – young and pretty and so recently widowed. People will start to talk."

"Really?" Emma asked, her hackles rising.

"I'm only telling you for your own good," Theresa said primly. "You're very young, you know."

"I would hope people would have better things to do than to spread unpleasant, untruthful gossip," Emma replied, very much on her dignity.

"So would I, but I doubt it, dear. People love a good gossip. I was only saying so to Doreen yesterday when we were talking about a story in the local newspaper this week – quite a shocking report, but I won't go into that now. I must be on my way."

Such was Emma's annoyance at this unwarranted interference that she simmered with irritation for the rest of the day and almost forgot her amusement at the irresistible adoption of Fred and Milo by an indefatigable do-gooder, although she did briefly think to hope that he would survive Theresa's cooking.

Over the ensuing days, her resentment slowly subsided

and she began to reflect that, however exasperating the manner of Theresa's admonition, there might be some justice in it. She knew that it was not only important to behave with integrity, but also to be seen to do so, in order to avoid bringing the gospel into disrepute.

She made up her mind to ask Janet whether anyone in their congregation might know of a reputable handyman and a gardener, whom she might engage on an occasional basis. Then, if Nick offered further assistance at any point in the future, she would be able to tell him that everything was under control.

CHAPTER 14

The twins had been a little tetchy for a day or two and by Tuesday Emma became certain that they were teething. They were wakeful at night and unsettled during the day. As a consequence, Emma found very little time to think of anything else. They chewed their little fists and dribbled continuously, they grizzled and fretted, their cheeks were flushed and their tempers frayed. Their weary mother, recalling with wry humour her recent assertion that she was managing perfectly well, took the precaution of acquiring some Calpol and a set of liquid-filled teething rings, which could be chilled for greater relief. She was glad that she had mastered the steriliser, as it came in useful for keeping the rings clean, even though she had not yet begun to use it for any other purpose.

She found that Millie and Joel were most likely to stop complaining for a while if she took them out in their pushchair so she walked a great deal, wheeling them around the local area to gain a little respite and getting to know a number of streets she had never been down before, but after a few days of this she was exhausted. On Friday night, the twins were painfully slow to settle to sleep and by one in the morning Joel was unhappily awake again. Emma admitted defeat and went to find the Calpol and a sterile spoon, reading the instructions twice through very carefully before she dared to administer the medicine. It took some time to have any effect, while she paced the floor, cradling Joel comfortingly and singing quietly to him, but eventually his cries ceased and she was at last able to lay him back in his cot.

She climbed thankfully back into her own rumpled bed and pulled the covers up but had barely started to relax when Millie began to wail. Wearily forcing herself back on to her feet, Emma repeated the procedure with her unhappy little daughter, rocked her until she settled and then put her gently down in her cot.

The babies slept soundly until morning, worn out by their crying and enjoying the beneficial effects of the medicine, but Emma spent much of the remainder of the night dozing intermittently, irrationally worrying that she might somehow have administered the wrong dosage to one of the twins and wondering how long this testing phase would last and whether it was better to get it all over with at once or whether it might have been preferable for them to take turns in growing their baby teeth. She thought the whole situation would not be so bad if only there were a time limit, a known period to the disruption, but faced with this wretchedness which could last days or even weeks, her heart quailed. She inclined her mind to prayer and asked God for respite and for strength and patience to continue to cope, and in the middle of her prayers she fell asleep, to be woken only a short while later by the twins' irritable demands for the day to begin.

Millie and Joel grumbled their way through the first part of the day and by half past nine in the morning were increasingly distressed. They had rejected their teething rings and were both building discernibly to a major eruption of bawling and Emma reluctantly decided she would have to resort to another dose of Calpol each.

Hastening up the stairs, followed by the twins' protests, she opened the bathroom cabinet where she kept the medicines and snatched at the bottle; but in her rush she misjudged the movement and the bottle slipped through her fingers, catching on the side of the bath as it fell and breaking, broadcasting sticky fluid far and wide. Emma could have wept with frustration. Not only was a major clean-up operation now required but any immediate prospect of calming the twins was also lost. As she stood gazing helplessly at the mess and listening to the twins cries from downstairs, she knew a moment of indecision as to which of her urgent problems to tackle first, but the powerful effect of her babies' distress very quickly led her to the inevitable conclusion that she should wheel them round to the pharmacy and purchase another bottle of Calpol as a matter of urgency.

She strapped the twins, still yelling, into their pushchair, grabbed her purse and opened the front door, to be greeted by unexpected the sight of Nick striding up the path towards her.

He stopped short. "You're going out," he remarked, plainly disconcerted.

"Yes, I have to," she replied curtly.

"Of course," he replied automatically. "It's just – I – er – I've got the washer for your tap. I'll come back another time – unless..."

"Unless?" Emma asked tersely over the twins' noise.

"I was wondering whether I could pop up and sort it anyway. I could let myself out when I've finished – if you're okay with that?"

Emma hesitated, reflecting that he had come all this way to help and what harm could it do? "Okay then," she agreed, but suddenly remembered the state of her bathroom. "Maybe not," she corrected herself, but realising that she must sound either rude or stupidly indecisive, she hastily tried to explain. "Erm, I had a bit of an accident – dropped a bottle of medicine. That's why I've got to go out – to buy a replacement."

"Are you ill? Would you like *me* to go and get the medicine?" he asked in quick concern.

"No, I'm fine. It's for the twins. But there's medicine all over the bathroom floor."

"Oh, I see. Don't worry – I'll clear it up. What's wrong with the twins?"

"Teeth!"

"At least it's not too serious."

"You wouldn't be saying that if you'd barely had a moment's rest for the last three days!" Emma said with some asperity.

"Sorry! Off you go then. I'll sort things out here."

Emma did not try to argue. Millie and Joel's demands were too insistent and she did not have enough energy to think of anything other than the pressing need to get to the chemist as quickly as possible.

Unfortunately, the local pharmacist recalled her recent visit and enquired rather disapprovingly into Emma's reasons for needing to buy another bottle of Calpol so soon. Once she had explained her carelessness, he reluctantly allowed her to make the purchase but, in the face of his evident though silent censure, she did not care to make the attempt to acquire a second bottle in case of further mishap, as she had planned to do.

On the walk home under an overcast sky, the twins napped uneasily and Emma began to think about Nick's visit. At least the neighbours could not imagine there was anything to gossip about so far, as she had been out since the moment of his arrival. She supposed she should not encourage him to linger once he had fixed the tap. Out of courtesy, she should probably offer him some refreshment and then send him on his way.

Reaching the house with the twins still asleep, Emma hoped to manoeuvre the pushchair indoors without disturbing them, but was speedily disabused of any such notion. As soon as the movement of the buggy changed, Millie and Joel woke and began to wail. There was no sign of Nick so she decided to focus on the twins' needs and only when she had given them both a dose of Calpol and comforted them until they at last grew calmer and she was able to get them back into their pushchair and rock it back and forth until they dropped off to sleep, did she feel able to seek him out.

In the bathroom she saw that order had been completely restored: the walls, bath and floor were clean and the fragments of broken bottle had all been removed. However, Nick was not there and the tap was still dripping. She called his name but there was no reply. She did not think he could have left; she had half-noticed what she thought was his blue car still parked at the kerbside as she had walked up the road. Slightly puzzled, she descended the stairs and called his name again, although not too loudly as she had no wish to disturb the twins. There was no answer, but his jacket was draped over the back of one of the kitchen chairs and she began to be aware of the drone of a motor outside so it occurred to her that he might have taken the opportunity to do some work on the garden. Sure enough, looking out of the kitchen window, she could see him busily trimming the hedge that bordered the end of the plot.

Now what was she to do? She could not go out and demand that he stop. Besides, she was so very tired: too tired for a confrontation. She would just sit down in the armchair for a minute and have a brief rest and *then* think about what to do next.

She slept.

CHAPTER 15

Waking gradually, Emma soon became conscious of a stiff neck which suggested that she had been asleep for some time. Pulling herself together, she went first to check on the twins, but they were still quietly slumbering so she felt able to go back to the kitchen, fill the kettle and switch it on. As she was dropping two teabags into the teapot, Nick looked in through the back door and saw that she was awake. He smiled and commented that he had checked on her and the twins a little while ago and found them all sleeping.

"Did *you* try the medicine too?" he asked flippantly.

Feeling unaccountably awkward at the idea that he might have watched her while she was asleep, Emma fixed her gaze on the teapot and asked whether he would like a drink.

"Tea would be great, please. I thought I'd give the lawn another trim next. It's grown a fair bit in the last fortnight but there's rain on the way so I need to get on with it." He disappeared as he spoke and Emma thought she might as well let him carry on. He had been here for a good while already. It seemed to her redundant as well as ungrateful to dismiss him now.

Once the pot had brewed, she took him a mug of tea

and a couple of biscuits on a tray. She admired the neat hedge and the tidily shaped shrubs, but did not linger.

Soon the twins were stirring again and she had her hands too full to consider the situation any further. She fed and changed them, buckled them into their bouncy chairs and gave them their teething rings, and began to think about what she might offer Nick for lunch. In the end, she settled for soup and rolls followed by an apple each and some fruitcake from a slab she had made the previous week, before this teething phase had caused so much havoc.

When the soup was hot, Emma called Nick in.

As he had previously, he began the meal very naturally with grace. He took the opportunity to pray for Emma and the twins and especially requested that the teething pain would quickly subside.

"Thank you," Emma said shyly after she had added her gentle 'Amen'.

"I guess teething is one of those inevitable stages that all babies have to go through," he remarked. "Do you have any idea how long it's likely to last?"

"It varies hugely between babies, but it *is* just a phase, as the saying goes."

"I imagine that's a saying that parents have to cling on to a lot in order to stay sane!"

Emma agreed and conversation ground to a halt.

Nick broke the silence by asking Emma whether she had heard about Ed's situation.

"Yes, and just when Charlie's pregnant again!"

"Ed didn't mention that to me," Nick said. "But then he probably wouldn't. Emma, I…" He hesitated and then resumed smoothly enough: "I'm sure they must be pleased – but I can see that it'll be an added stress for them at a time like this. I-I found out yesterday that there might be a couple of vacancies in the accounts department at my firm, so I thought I might call round on Ed when I've finished here and let him know."

"I'm sure he'd be very grateful," Emma remarked. She was convinced that he had been about to say something different and had changed his mind, but she did not feel able to question him: their relationship was not relaxed enough for that.

They discussed Ed and Charlie's circumstances for a little longer and then silence fell again. Emma racked her brain for something to say and remembered Theresa Halton's account of the way she had assumed responsibility for her neighbour. She relayed this to Nick, who enjoyed the story a great deal, but suggested - only half in jest - that she call on Fred sometime to check that he was happy with developments.

By the time they had finished eating, Millie was demanding some attention, so Nick picked her up and found various ways to divert her while Emma cleared the table and put things away. It wasn't long before Joel added his complaints to his sister's and Emma supposed that the effects of the medication must be wearing off. She was reluctant to administer any more medicine before bedtime and resigned herself to a trying afternoon.

Nick offered further assistance but Emma suggested uncomfortably that perhaps he ought to be going soon, if he was to see Ed before it got too late in the day. What she meant was that he would need to see Ed soon if he was not to arrive home so late that he upset Penny, but she couldn't quite bring herself to say that, in case it led to difficult explanations.

"If you're sure you're okay, I'll finish the lawn and tidy up," Nick said, passing Millie over. "Then I'll just fit that new washer and go round and see Ed."

Emma found that the twins were not as miserable as she had feared and with judicious entertainment she kept them distracted and amused for some time. Passing through on his way to fix the tap, Nick commented that they were looking rather sleepy and, studying them properly, Emma realised that he was right. She had been so certain that their sore gums would keep them awake and miserable that she had missed the signs. Their long rest before lunch would not necessarily prevent them from sleeping again now, since their night had been very wakeful. She elected to lay them down in their cots and see whether they would settle, thinking that she would take her chances with any variation in their usual routine since their sleep patterns had already been so disrupted in recent days.

Both Millie and Joel protested briefly at being put in their cots, but their whimpers soon subsided and Emma was able to switch the monitor on and go back down to the kitchen. She took a bundle of washing down with her and, having sorted through it, was loading the washing machine when Nick reappeared, saying cheerfully that the tap was now as good as new.

Emma thanked him, picking up the laundry detergent bottle as she did so and starting to unscrew the cap.

Nick glanced at his watch and said hesitantly: "Look, I'd better go, if I'm going to see Ed, but I – could we – have a chat sometime?"

Emma dropped the lid of the bottle.

"A chat?" she asked apprehensively.

"Yes," Nick said, picking the lid up and returning it to her. "I – there are things I think we – need to discuss."

She placed the bottle and cap carefully on the work surface and looked up at him doubtfully, but before she could formulate a question, he had taken her chin in a firm clasp and bent and kissed her full on the lips. For a moment, she was too surprised to react but then, amidst the torrent of confused emotions tumbling through her, she remembered not only her anger against this man but Sam and Penny as well, and she stiffened and pulled away.

"Don't!" she cried. "Don't touch me!"

He released her immediately.

"Emma -," he began awkwardly, but she was not prepared to listen. She was burning to unburden herself of the years of suppressed hurt and resentment.

"How dare you!" she burst out. "You waltz in here as if you can just ignore the past, but you've never once apologised for the way you treated me all those years ago. I ought to hate you for that. And you haven't changed, have you? You conveniently forget Penny - and Sam. I'm a *widow*. Up till three or so months ago, Sam was my *husband* – Millie and Joel's *father*! This is all wrong."

"But what has -?"

"Please just go!" She turned away.

"Won't you at least let me explain?"

"*No!*" Emma exclaimed forcefully - desperately, refusing to look at him. "Please go! And don't – don't come back!" she finished wretchedly.

He picked up his jacket and moved reluctantly towards the door.

"Goodbye then," he said, painstakingly expressionless.

Emma did not move or speak so he let himself out, closing the door to the hall behind him with extreme care. A few seconds later she heard the front door close softly.

Once she was sure he had gone, she allowed herself to weep.

She should never have let him into the house. She should have followed her conscience and told him that it was not right for him to visit, but she had been weak-willed and selfish. She had been glad of the practical help he offered and, she was compelled to admit, glad of his company.

For an instant, when he had kissed her, she had almost responded, and the vehemence of her subsequent reaction owed something to the shame she felt at the realisation that she still found him attractive - after all that had happened, despite her marriage to Sam and the knowledge that Nick was in some way committed to another woman.

What on earth had prompted him to kiss her? Was it simply a passing whim? She wondered for a moment whether he could still have feelings for her but presumed bitterly that, at most, he must only feel desire. She knew, for she had repeatedly told herself so, that he could not love her, had never loved her, or he could not have treated her as he had six years ago. Manifestly, he was a man without principles. She had feared that to be living with one woman and to spend significant time with another must be wrong but she had not suspected him of any improper intentions. Now, however, he had revealed himself to be entirely lacking in integrity. How had he supposed she would react to such insulting and immoral behaviour?

Well, now she had finally told him what she thought of him – in part, at any rate. She had done the right thing, honoured Sam's memory and protected Penny's interests. She had sent him away and told him to stay away. She supposed she would never see him again. The tears streamed down her cheeks and she did not know why she was crying. Was it because she felt so dreadful for failing to think of Sam for that brief, crucial moment, was it because her disillusionment with Nick was painfully complete, or was it grief at the recognition that, had his character not been so gravely flawed, Nick could have been such a wonderful person?

She could not help wondering what he had thought there was to discuss. Had he intended to revisit the past or to talk about his present situation or had he had something else in mind altogether? Had it just been a ploy to give him a reason for another visit? She had been completely justified in refusing to hear him out or to encourage him in any way. His behaviour had been unforgivable.

CHAPTER 16

Millie and Joel slept on for about half an hour longer and then woke one after the other in a perfectly good humour. Emma breathed a sigh of relief and offered up grateful thanks to the Lord for this respite. She still felt crushed by the recollection of what had taken place between her and Nick and drained by the events of recent days, and a little lull in the more challenging demands of motherhood was hugely welcome.

The remainder of the day passed without incident. The twins seemed restored to their usual sunny equanimity and, although bedtime was a little later than normal because of the length of their afternoon nap, there was no sign that they were experiencing any further discomfort.

The twins passed a restful night but Emma was not so blessed. Despite her fatigue, she could not sleep. Her brain kept presenting her with memories: clear pictures of the afternoon's events, which made her writhe with mortification, and other recollections from her past – memories of encounters with Nick both recent and historical, and memories of Sam.

She felt somehow more inconsolably lonely than ever, more aware that the responsibility for Millie and Joel must fall to herself alone. Depression overwhelmed her and she cried desolate tears into her pillow.

As she wallowed in this intense misery, she heard a small voice inside her head saying almost tauntingly, "What happened to your conviction of God's goodness? That didn't last long, did it?"

Her first instinct was to make excuses, to justify herself on the grounds of exhaustion, grief, exceptional circumstances, the twins' indisposition, Nick's unforgivable behaviour. However, her reason told her that if God was good, then God was *always* good, despite all those aforementioned justifications. Just because she could not see the good, that did not mean that there was no good. The interaction between people's suffering and God's goodness was beyond human comprehension but the Bible confidently asserted that suffering could produce good fruit in a believer and that even when men committed evil deeds God could use it for good. This was shown clearly, for example, in the life of Joseph and supremely in the death of Jesus, who was crucified with the help of wicked men but 'by God's set purpose and foreknowledge' for the salvation of many.

Reminded of these great truths, Emma at last began to pray and, having turned back to God, she soon slept.

The improvement in the twin's health and humour appeared to be maintained the following morning and, with an enormous sense of reprieve, Emma fed them, dressed them and got ready for church.

She was still struggling to come to terms with the events of the previous day and to pardon herself for her own part in them; she still felt the hurt and betrayal of Nick's offence like a weight on her heart, but she was eager to get to St

Anthony's to hear God's word and her efforts were rewarded by an uplifting service and a thought-provoking and highly apposite sermon from the vicar, Michael, on the topic of forgiveness.

He took as his main text the line from the Lord's prayer: 'Forgive us our sins as we forgive those who sin against us,' which he unpacked in the context of the parable of the unforgiving debtor. Emma understood the implication. We have each, through God's great grace and mercy, been forgiven so much that we should overflow with joy and gratitude, which should be shown by a willingness to extend forgiveness to others. Indeed, if we find ourselves unable to pardon others, we must ask ourselves whether we have really understood God's amazing, free gift of forgiveness and redemption.

This spoke directly to Emma's tender conscience and her thoughts strayed as she wondered how she could begin to forgive Nick for all that he had done to injure her and destroy her peace of mind. It was easy enough to say that you forgave someone but to mean it was rather more of a challenge. How could she reach the point where she no longer kept account of his misdeeds? Since she had standards and expectations, she was bound to notice when others failed to live up to them. But perhaps it was not so much that she should not notice their deficiencies in the first place but that she should be more aware that she, like everyone else, was an abject sinner before a holy God. She tried to consider Nick in those terms but the hurt was too recent, too raw, too incomprehensible, and she could not bring herself to the point of accepting that she was as much a sinner as he was. Clearly, she was going to have to work at that.

She brought her attention back to Michael's talk and found that he was acknowledging that sometimes it could be very difficult to forgive, when the pain caused by someone else's sin was particularly deep. He suggested the need to remember Jesus' crucifixion. "At the cross," he said, "Jesus suffered both physical agony and total abandonment and yet he cried out to God to forgive those who abused and killed him. So when he commands us to follow his example and forgive others, he knows what he is asking. And don't forget that he doesn't expect us to do it in our own strength. He offers healing and comfort, if we allow Him to work in our hearts. Of course, you can't expect forgiveness to happen instantly. It may take much time and prayer. And I want to be clear that forgiveness is not about suggesting that sin is understandable or acceptable in any way. Quite the reverse. It is popular these days to blame one's upbringing, one's genes, one's environment, but sin is still sin and forgiveness doesn't play down either the sin or its terrible consequences. Instead, forgiveness allows you to say: 'I *have* been ill-treated, but I will not let the experience affect the rest my life; I *have* been hurt but I will not let the pain harden my heart. I will not hold tightly to my resentment. I will give it to the Lord and allow him to work, trusting in his goodness and justice.'"

Emma bowed her head and prayed fervently, asking the Lord to bring her to the point where she could let go of her resentment and hand it over to Him. She did not feel any immediate sense of release but was glad to have had her thoughts clarified and to have an aim, a direction for her prayers.

After the service, she caught sight of Charlie, Ed and little Dan and, without reflecting that it might lead to awkward questions, went to ask what they thought of the news of the vacancies at Nick's firm.

Ed looked puzzled. "What vacancies?"

"Didn't Nick call round yesterday?"

"No," Ed replied doubtfully.

"Oh!" Emma was baffled. "He said he would. He dropped round to fix one of my taps and he was planning to call on you afterwards. Were you out?"

Emma saw the effort with which Ed and Charlie did not exchange glances and she wished she had kept quiet about Nick's visit.

"We were in all day," Charlie said.

"Perhaps he ran out of time," Emma suggested hurriedly. "I'm sure he'll be in touch."

"Can you tell us what he's planning to say?" Ed asked with his customary calm.

"He'd heard that there might be a couple of vacancies in the accounts department of his company. He thought you might be interested."

Ed looked suddenly attentive. "I'll ring Nick later," he told Charlie soothingly and then pursued Dan in the direction of the biscuits and squash.

Noticing that her friend was rather pale, Emma asked how she was feeling.

"A bit rough," came the resigned reply. "But I expect it'll wear off after a few weeks. How about you? You look exhausted."

"We've just had a bout of teething – Millie and Joel simultaneously – so I'm rather short of sleep."

"Poor you! Are they better now?"

"They seem to be."

"So Nick fixed a tap for you yesterday," Charlie remarked casually. "Has he been helping out much?"

"Only a couple of times," Emma replied with considerable reserve. "Once when he brought that casserole you'd kindly sent and then on one other occasion, when he did a bit of gardening." She instinctively played down his contribution, lest Charlie should gain the wrong impression, particularly as there was the chance that she or Ed might say something to Penny at some point.

"He's kind, isn't he?" Charlie said.

"Mmm." Emma was noncommittal.

"What do you make of him these days?" her friend persisted.

"He hasn't changed much," Emma replied. "And by that I mean he hasn't changed for the better!" she added waspishly.

Charlie looked taken aback but little Dan returned at that point with a half-eaten custard cream, followed imperturbably but closely by Ed, and the topic was dropped.

At parting, Charlie asked whether Emma wanted to arrange to meet up during the week, but Emma excused herself from making any commitment on the grounds that she had forgotten her diary and wasn't quite sure when she would be free. The truth was that she was reluctant to expose herself to any more inquiries about Nick. Setting aside the general awkwardness of the topic, Emma was especially wary because Charlie knew all about Nick's treachery six years ago and had comforted and supported her friend at that time. She would think Emma had lost her wits if she learnt that she had allowed herself to be hurt by him again.

By the time Charlie rang the following day to pursue

the possibility of meeting up, Emma had been able to give the matter some thought and she strategically suggested that they invite along another woman from church who had recently announced that she was expecting her first child. "I'm pretty sure Liz will be around," Emma said. "Because she's a teacher and it's the summer holidays. It might be good to be friendly and include her. What do you think?"

"Good idea," Charlie replied good-naturedly, as Emma had guessed she would. "It's not always an easy transition from working to being at home with a baby and it might help her if she gets to know a few of us better first."

They agreed to meet at Charlie's house for morning coffee and the get-together went well; Liz seemed to appreciate the invitation as well as the opportunity to ask questions and to observe the three available specimens of infanthood. Charlie never suspected that Liz was Emma's protection against difficult questions and the ploy was certainly effective.

They discussed all sorts of vital issues such as delivery options, varieties of nappy, sleep routines and feeding. Emma had just begun to introduce the twins to formula milk, with no ill effects, but could not add a great deal to the conversation at this point as she had only tried one type of milk so far and that for only a few days. She could report with satisfaction, however, that the twins were making the transition to the bottle without objection. She also explained that as the twins were now six months old - to the day - she intended to try them with some apple puree at lunchtime and gradually introduce other soft cooked fruit and vegetables followed by finger foods.

"Six months old!" exclaimed Charlie. "Goodness me, how time flies by!"

"Yes, when you look back, it feels as though it's gone in a flash," Emma agreed. "But when you're coping with any particular phase, it can seem like a lifetime! Those first weeks of sleepless nights and endless feeding and nappy changing – and having no idea when they're going to settle into any kind of routine – were the longest weeks of my life."

"I thought that too," Charlie agreed. "And I only had one to cope with."

"We have a history of twins in my family," Liz remarked. "And I must say, I was quite relieved when the scan showed that I was only expecting one baby. Was it a complete surprise to you to find that you were carrying two?"

"Yes, but a *wonderful* surprise. My husband was so ecstatic – and so proud when they were born. It's good to remember that now he's gone. And I think it will be a blessing in the future for the two of them to have each other."

"We must always count our blessings," Charlie said seriously, and Liz concurred.

Simply because Emma had avoided cross-questioning by her friend, it did not mean that she gave Nick no further thought. In fact, he was in her thoughts all too often. So many things seemed to remind her of him.

Every time she entered her bathroom and saw that the tap no longer dripped, every time she looked out at her tidy back garden with its colourful bushes of cistus and spirea flowering abundantly and the neat clumps of hardy geranium and pink and white valerian, she remembered his kindness; but then she would also recall his transgressions and wonder again how anyone so thoughtful could also behave so badly.

She told herself that it was because she was shocked by his inexplicable behaviour that she so frequently found herself rehearsing his iniquities. She also found herself trying to guess with repetitive obsessiveness why he had kissed her. Had it just been the impulse of the moment? She thought that men were often driven by compulsions which were incomprehensible to her, but on every view it seemed to her extraordinary.

She tried very hard to put Michael's preaching into practice and to hand over the task of judgement of Nick's actions and motives to God, but just when she imagined she was making some progress with letting go of her anger, her thoughts would betray her and she would find herself in the old cycle of confusion and resentment. She longed to understand Nick but, despite much reflection, was no nearer to solving the riddle of his character and conduct.

Thinking that she might benefit from reminding herself of the extent of God's goodness, faithfulness and justice, Emma went on a hunt through the Bible, with the help of a concordance, and located verses to which she could turn in times of stress. She found many that were helpful but the one to which she returned most often and which she wrote on a card and put up on her fridge was from Proverbs: 'Trust in the Lord with all your heart and lean not on your own understanding; in all your ways acknowledge him, and he will make your paths straight.'

CHAPTER 17

Millie and Joel took instantly and eagerly to apple puree. Pear puree was greeted with equal enthusiasm; carrot was not quite as popular. Emma enjoyed experimenting with different cooked fruit and vegetables and observing the twins' reactions, the expressions on their faces and their interest in each new taste and texture. She felt that they were making real and steady progress but her pleasure was diminished by having no one to share it with.

Analysing her dissatisfaction, she concluded that, although she was becoming more accustomed to life without Sam and had accepted the inescapable fact that he was gone, she would always miss the support of knowing that there was one person who was interested in the minutiae of her existence. She wondered whether she would ever find someone to fill that gap in her life.

After church the following Sunday, Emma learnt from Ed that he had been in contact with Nick and, as the vacancies at his firm had not yet been advertised, had submitted a speculative application for any kind of accountancy role within the company.

"Thanks for the tip-off," Ed added. "Nick said he'd intended to call round, but something had cropped up and it had temporarily slipped his mind. He sounded a bit preoccupied. Have you heard from him at all this week?"

Emma thought he was watching her rather closely and instantly and unequivocally denied any communication, while wondering whether he was beginning to suspect something. She desperately wanted to prevent any hint of what had happened getting back to Penny as she was eager to avoid causing her any distress.

She made a concerted effort to appear cheerful and adopted a falsely jaunty, chatty manner, which seemed to reassure Ed, although Charlie was unconvinced and regarded her friend with a little concern. She twice enquired whether Emma was alright and reminded her to phone if she could help in any way or even if she just wanted a chat.

Emma smiled brightly and told Charlie that she was fine, willing it to be true for, after all, how could she begin to admit the confusion of her feelings, the guilt she felt over the realisation that she had, however briefly, allowed herself to contemplate the possibility that she might one day find another life companion, the soul-searching over any trouble she might have caused Penny, the bitterness of her attitude towards Nick.

Had she not been coping with the fluctuations of morning sickness, Charlie might have pursued the matter further, but her own discomfort precluded her from giving her friend's difficulties her full attention. She did resolve that if Emma did not call her, she would phone her friend in a few days' time to see whether she seemed any more at ease.

The following evening, Emma had just taken Millie and Joel upstairs for their bath, when the doorbell rang. Popping

Millie in her cot for safety, she went back downstairs carrying Joel in his nappy and little button-through vest.

Opening the front door, she discovered a vaguely familiar, dark-haired girl standing there in the shadows.

"Yes? Can I help you?" Emma asked.

The young lady stepped forward and Emma recognised her as she spoke shyly: "Hello! I'm Penny – perhaps you don't remember me?"

"Oh yes. *Now* I do," Emma replied, puzzled at this unexpected visit. "If you're looking for Nick," she added rather defensively, "he's not here."

"I didn't think he would be. May I – may I come in for a minute?"

"Of course," Emma replied politely but with considerable reluctance. She led the way into the sitting room, wondering whether she was about to be treated to an emotional scene.

"Do take a seat," she went on with some reserve. "I'll put Joel in his chair and then I'd better go and fetch Millie."

She strapped Joel into his chair, while he kicked and wriggled, and gave him a toy to clutch, very conscious of Penny's eyes on her as she did so.

"I'll be right back," she added, nerves on edge, as she headed for the stairs.

When she returned, carrying a cheery Millie, she found Penny disarmingly on her knees beside Joel's bouncy chair, handing back the toy he had discarded and chatting to him, her smooth sable hair swinging across her cheek. She looked up and smiled gently at Emma and Millie.

"Aren't they sweet!" she exclaimed. "I remember when my nieces and nephews were this age: so cute!"

"I'm afraid they're not always this cheerful," Emma said ruefully. "They're not so sweet when they're yelling."

"Oh, I know," Penny acknowledged. "Having twins must be an enormous amount of work."

"It has its moments," Emma smiled, sitting down with Millie on her lap and thinking that this was a very strange conversation to be having with this girl.

"Yes, so Nick mentioned."

"I presume it's about Nick that you've come to see me?" Emma asked with some hardihood.

"Yes. He's so unhappy I made up my mind to speak to you, but now I'm here I don't know what to say," Penny confessed shyly, tucking her dark hair behind an ear in a way that conveyed her uncertainty.

"It's alright," Emma said, controlling her voice with an effort as she sought to reassure the younger girl. "Last time he was here, I told him not to come back again."

"Then that's why he's wretched. Did you know that he'd started looking for accommodation over this way? He's dropped that now – I heard him calling the letting agents this morning to cancel his registration."

"And you were okay with that?" Emma asked, amazed and confused.

"With what?"

"With him planning to move out?"

"It's been nice having him to stay, of course, but it was only ever meant to be a temporary arrangement. I encouraged him to think about moving over this way. I thought everything might work out beautifully for him. He's had such a difficult time and he's a great brother. I – I just wanted him to be happy."

Brother! Emma was left speechless; she could hardly believe what she had heard: Nick and Penny were brother and sister! What an astounding revelation! But that is certainly what Penny had said so it must be true. Suddenly, everything fell into place; and, although it was not very obvious, she could even see the likeness between them now she searched for it.

"I – I'm sorry," Penny added humbly, unsure in the face of the prolonged silence. "Perhaps I shouldn't have come."

Through her stupefaction, Emma felt it was incumbent on her to respond to the appeal in Penny's voice.

"Why –" she began, but found she had to clear her throat before she could continue. "Why do you say he's had a difficult time?"

"Well, you know – everything that's happened – his health problems..." Realising that Emma was looking mystified she tailed off miserably. "I'd better not say any more," she went on after a moment. "But please could you at least speak to him. I – I don't know why you sent him away and I don't mean to pry but I hate to see him as down as he's been for the last week or so."

"You must be very fond of your brother, to come all the way over here to see me."

"Of course. You must be fond of your brother too," Penny added diffidently.

"Luke? Yes, he's kind – and very generous – but he can't be around much."

"Does he keep in touch?" Penny asked, holding a toy out for Joel.

"Not regularly, but when he has time. He visited me

when he was in the UK last month and I think he's planning another visit soon, which will be nice."

Penny assented and gave her full attention to Joel for a little while, before getting to her feet and saying that she should leave.

"I appreciate your visit," Emma said with real gratitude. "I'm sorry – I haven't offered you any refreshments," she added suddenly becoming aware of the oversight.

"Don't worry. You've got your hands full. Is there anything I can do to help before I go?"

Emma declined the kind offer thinking that it seemed to be a family trait to offer help so readily but that Penny would be late enough home as it was.

They made their farewells and Emma repeated her thanks for the visit. "Perhaps we can meet up again sometime," she said.

"I hope so," Penny replied, with a blush. She seemed to be about to add something more but must have had second thoughts.

Pondering over the unexpected visit, Emma thought that Penny seemed a sweet girl, and very pretty. She had been as unaffectedly friendly towards the babies as her brother had always been. Emma was very glad that she had not betrayed her foolish notion that Penny was Nick's girlfriend. That would have been extremely embarrassing.

It was embarrassing enough as it was. How could she have made such a ridiculous mistake?

She tried to recall what Nick had said when he had introduced her to his attractive companion after Sam's service, but the encounter was shrouded in the haze which seemed to have dogged her for most of that dreadful day.

She had not forgotten her anger at his presence there and she also remembered seeing Penny put her arm around her brother as he had walked away and the loneliness which had washed over her as she had watched them go.

If only she had noticed their family likeness or recalled any of the details of Nick's many siblings, she might have avoided the pain of such a foolish misunderstanding, but six years is a long time and she had not fully mastered the complications of Nick's family at the time of their association, let alone made any attempt to remember them subsequently.

Thinking through the implications of what she had just learnt, Emma realised that one strand of her resentment against Nick had completely given way. He had not been living with one woman and hoping to charm another. He had not been deceitful or immoral.

So why had he called round to help her? And why, *why* had he kissed her? Was he still fond of her? Her foolish heart leaped at the notion until she sternly subdued it, reminding herself fiercely of his past betrayal. It was possible, she thought reflectively, that he had at some point regretted his former decision to cast her off and, when he discovered that she was free once more, had thought to pursue her, but if he imagined that, now it suited him better, he could pick up where he had left off six years ago he was sadly mistaken. She was glad – very glad – that she had not encouraged him, had not succumbed to his kiss. What kind of weakling did he think she was to assume that she would fall into his arms if he showed her a little kindness?

Penny thought he was miserable and that it might help if she spoke to him, but she had no intention of contacting him. He could not possibly be as miserable as she had been six years ago when he had discarded her so abruptly, although it would serve him right if he were. If he was vainly hoping that she might call, it was nothing more than he deserved for all those calls and pleas of hers that he had left unheeded.

She wondered, as she had once before, whether he had had many girlfriends since their breakup and resolved to ask Charlie sometime.

Thinking about Charlie, Emma realised that she and Ed must know that Nick and Penny were brother and sister. So what was the import of their recent meaningful looks and tentatively probing questions? Did they wonder whether Nick was interested in some way? Perhaps Nick had even confessed as much. Charlie certainly knew all about Nick's past unreliability and must have shared what she knew with her husband, so no doubt Ed and Charlie were concerned that Emma might be hurt again by him. Well, they need not worry – she had no intention of being taken in by him a second time.

Although… he had been very kind and thoughtful in calling round and helping unpretentiously with jobs in the house and garden. He had been very good with the twins. What if he had seen the error of his ways over the years and had become a reformed character? Could that be possible? Could she ever trust him? No, it was ridiculous – and far too soon after Sam's passing to be considering it, however idly. She would think no more about it. But she recalled suddenly that she had stopped Charlie rather brusquely when she had begun to volunteer an assessment of Nick's present character and, if an opportunity arose, she thought she might just prompt Charlie to give her opinion after all.

CHAPTER 18

Tuesday was the day scheduled for Rachel's visit with her three children. Emma had been making gradual preparations in recent days and, in addition to cleaning and tidying rather more thoroughly than usual, she had bought most of the ingredients she needed for the meal they were to share.

She had decided to cook chicken fillets with plain pasta and to offer a simple tomato and basil sauce for those who wanted it. She hoped that would accommodate all the different restrictions listed by her sister. She planned to cook some frozen peas for her nieces and nephew but she wanted to offer a fresh side salad for the adults, at least, so she strapped Millie and Joel into their pushchair on Tuesday morning and set off in the bright, summer sunshine to the nearest supermarket to choose a selection of salad leaves and other ingredients. While she was there, she also bought some bananas and avocado to vary the twins' diet and found two desserts – one lemon and one chocolate – which she hoped would appeal to all her visitors' tastes. Failing that, she had made a sponge cake the day before, which might be an acceptable alternative.

On her way home, Emma decided on the spur of the moment to walk along Wallace Road. When she reached number thirty-two, she stopped and looked at the neatly paved, but rather soulless front garden, wondering whether to knock on the front door and introduce herself. As she stood there, the door opened and, to her surprise, Theresa hailed her.

"I thought it was you, dear. Come along in and say hello to Fred and Milo."

"I can't really stop," Emma excused herself. "I've got shopping that needs to go in the fridge."

"Just come in for a moment" Theresa decreed. "Fred would love to meet you."

Emma had begun to wheel the pushchair up to the doorstep when a series of shrill barks alerted her to the swift emergence from the house of the little terrier she had last seen tearing around her back garden. He seemed equally excited on this occasion so perhaps all his life was lived at a high-energy level of eager curiosity and enjoyment. He raced round the front garden, yapping and jumping, his tail wagging so fast it was almost a blur. Barley followed more sedately and came over to sniff at the pushchair and at the shopping stowed away underneath. Emma was glad that all her purchases were protected by wrappers or bags.

A few seconds later a small, slight, white-haired gentleman appeared on the doorstep, leaning on a stick.

"Good morning," he said courteously and Theresa made the introductions.

"Ah, so you are the good angel to whom I owe my acquaintance with this wonderful lady," Fred said to Emma in his quavering voice. "And these are your twins. Splendid."

Theresa beamed complacently and called Milo and Barley over to her for a pat.

"I'm glad you are enjoying the – um – unsolicited

acquaintance," Emma said, with the hint of a question in her tone.

"Oh yes, Theresa looks after me so carefully: I haven't been so well fed for years. And Milo, who is rather a handful as you can see, has great fun with dear old Barley. We were just thinking about taking them out for a walk but I'm not too steady on my pins this morning."

"I'm sorry," Emma said gently. "If there's ever anything I can do, you know I'm just over the back hedge. Perhaps I could give you my number?"

Theresa bridled a little and Fred said tactfully, "This dear lady seems to have it all in hand."

"Yes, indeed," Theresa said authoritatively. "You'd best stay at home, Fred, if you're feeling a bit wobbly. I'll take the dogs out and pop to the chemist for your prescription while I'm about it."

"That would be very good of you," Fred said, ever civil, and nodded to Emma. "If you don't mind, I'll go back and sit down."

"Of course," she replied. "Lovely to meet you."

"Wait a minute, dear," Theresa said to Emma, "and I'll walk with you to the end of the road."

She disappeared indoors.

Emma waited obediently while the twins watched the antics of the two dogs with great interest.

Theresa emerged shortly from the house with her handbag and leads for the dogs. She had a little difficulty persuading Milo to stand still for long enough to be able to attach the lead to his collar but soon they were off.

"I'm glad of this opportunity to have a little word,"

Theresa said confidentially. "I was thinking of dropping round. I've got a favour to ask, if I may?"

"What is it?" Emma asked, trying not to sound too wary.

"You see that Fred is very frail. He doesn't get out much and he can't walk far. I think he'd like to get to church on Sunday – he hasn't been for years, he says – and, as you live so near, I wondered whether you could give him a lift. I don't drive – never have – and taxis are very dear."

"I'd be happy to," Emma replied, relieved that this was a request she could grant without significantly exposing herself or the twins to Theresa's lax notions of health and hygiene.

"If you call round at nine thirty, I'll make sure I'm there to help get Fred into the car and lock up the house properly for him. That'll give us plenty of time to get to the church and get Fred comfortable before ten. You won't mind giving me a lift as well; I'll be fine squeezing in the back seat between the twins."

And so it was agreed. They parted company at the corner and Emma wheeled the pushchair the rest of the way home, wondering whether she had committed herself to a one-off arrangement or whether Fred would like to get to church every week. Not that it mattered: she would be glad to help such an elderly gentleman.

Back at home, Emma quickly put her purchases away and then extracted the twins from the pushchair. There were hours yet before she need think about her sister's arrival and the day was so glorious that she decided to take the playpen out into the back garden and see whether she could make a bit more progress with uprooting some of the ever-abundant weeds.

As she had done on previous occasions, she established the twins in the comfort of the playpen with a variety of entertainments, went to find her gardening tools and set to work.

Looking round the garden with its bright, summer hues, she was reminded again of Nick's visits and of his many kindnesses, and her thoughts turned to Penny's half-revelations of the night before. She had said something about her brother having had a 'difficult time' and had mentioned health problems. Emma turned these morsels over in her mind, wondering exactly what they meant and trying to see whether they had any bearing on Nick's present situation and possible intentions. If he had been seriously ill, might he have had an opportunity to reflect on his past life and have learnt to feel regret and remorse for his treatment of her? How she wished she had access to all the facts.

And that was when it struck her: the last time she had seen him he had said there were things he wanted to discuss! Perhaps he had been about to speak of those intervening years and his current hopes. But then he had kissed her and she had refused to have anything more to do with him, had refused to listen to his plea to be allowed to explain. She had been so confused by his apparent relationship with Penny that she had rejected the opportunity to learn the very facts she now longed to hear. How she regretted her misunderstanding of Penny's role in his life.

She tackled a particularly robust dandelion and dug up as much of the root as she could grasp, wishing it were as easy to deal with the disorder of her own emotions as it was to weed a flowerbed. Despite Penny's entreaty that she speak to Nick, Emma couldn't see how she could possibly phone him out of the blue and solicit the explanation she had previously refused to hear. That would take a great deal more nerve than she possessed, and he might refuse to have anything to do with her – as he had once before. The best she could think of was to phone Charlie sometime and see whether she could obtain any clarification from her.

Inevitably, Emma had to abandon the weeding after a while to amuse Millie and Joel, but she was able to return to it for another stint after lunch. She made sure she cleared up and was back indoors with the twins in good time to be ready for her sister's arrival and was holding Joel and watching from the front window, while Millie played happily on the rug, when Rachel's large, shiny four-wheel drive pulled up outside the house in the late afternoon and disgorged three bouncing children and their elegant mother.

Emma went and set the front door welcomingly wide and a few moments later her hallway was full of visitors.

"Come through," she urged them, directing them towards the kitchen and following with Joel, whom she buckled into his highchair at the kitchen table. When she had fetched Millie and strapped her safely into her highchair, she offered her visitors refreshments. The children were looking round this new location with open curiosity but they eagerly requested a drink of water each and Jago asked whether there were any biscuits.

"Chocolate are my favourite," he confided.

"Mine too," Emma smiled. She looked questioningly at her sister. "Are they allowed a biscuit?"

"Just one each," Rachel replied in minatory tones, seating herself at the kitchen table.

To the children's delight, Emma opened a packet of bourbon biscuits. She also handed them each a cup of water, before switching the kettle on to make tea for the adults. The children finished their drinks and biscuits in a matter of moments, so Rachel suggested that they go out in the garden and run off some steam, after having been in the car for so long. Emma obligingly opened the back door for them and Jago disappeared outside in a flash, but Tillie and Clemmie hung back saying there was nothing to do outside.

"Well, you can't have your phones," their mother told them defensively. "You've been playing on them for the whole car journey and you'll want them on the plane later. Some fresh air will do you good."

"Can't we stay here and play with the babies?" Tilly asked pleadingly and Clemmie nodded vigorously.

"Only if you're very good and quiet," Rachel warned them. "Mummy and Auntie Emma want to have a chat."

"I tell you what," Emma said kindly to the girls. "If you go and look in the front room – the one we came past when we came through the hall – you'll find a box of toys and books. You can choose a few to bring back to show Millie and Joel. They'd really like that."

Tilly and Clemmie skipped off and their high, childish voices could soon be heard commenting on the contents of the toy box.

"Well, Emma," said her sister commandingly, as Emma poured the tea. "Tell me how you've been getting on. You look as though you've been rather letting yourself go, if you don't mind my saying so."

"I've been gardening," Emma explained.

"That might justify the outfit and your hair being bundled up so untidily, but you've lost too much weight and – no make-up – *really*?"

"Are appearances that important?" Emma asked pleasantly, passing her sister a mug and dropping into her usual seat between the twins, cradling her own mug between her hands. "What about 'the unfading beauty of a gentle and quiet spirit, which is of great worth in God's sight'?"

"Where does that come from?"

"The Bible – one of Peter's letters."

"It's all very well, but you ought to have some standards. After all, it's everyone else who has to look at you."

Emma laughed and Rachel looked cross.

"I'm sorry," Emma said. "But it's ridiculous, you know."

"What's ridiculous?"

"Worrying about my appearance. Most of the time there's no one here to see or care."

"*I'm* here."

"I'm sorry if I offend your sensibilities."

"It's not that exactly, but someone has to tell you."

"Why?"

"So you know what everyone's thinking."

"I don't think you can presume to speak for everyone," Emma pointed out mildly. "Look, let's not quarrel. I'll agree that I've let myself go if you'll concede that there are more important things to think about."

"Yes, but not if you want to find another man."

"But –"

Rachel held up a hand. "I know! I know it's early days,"

she interjected. "But you must admit that the twins could do with a father figure."

Emma glanced at her babies, sitting blithely in their highchairs, and could think of nothing polite to say in response.

"And what you have to realise," her sister went on officiously, "is that they will be a considerable handicap to finding another man. As Harry says, there are not many men who'll be keen to saddle themselves with another chap's little twins. It's a lot to ask. You might have to settle for a widower or a divorcee."

As Emma drew breath to tell her sister in no uncertain terms to mind her own business, Tilly and Clemmie reappeared with an armful of toys each, and she was obliged to hold her tongue. She was so angry that she had to stand up and walk away from the table for a moment. She put her mug in the dishwasher and switched the oven on so that it could begin to warm up, simply for an excuse to have something to do, but she was soon appealed to by Tilly, who wanted to know whether their cousins liked listening to stories, and then by Clemmie, who asked whether the babies could talk.

By the time she had dealt with these enquiries and encouraged the girls to show their selection of toys to Millie and Joel, she had got her temper under control, although she could not resist saying sarcastically to her sister, "Does Harry have any other good advice?"

Her barb missed its mark, however, as Rachel took the question at face value and proceeded to pass on various pearls of wisdom about where she might meet a second husband and how she might try to ensure that the twins did not appear to be too great a deterrent.

"I suppose Harry doesn't think I might meet someone at church?" Emma asked.

"Oh, I know you met Sam at church," Rachel said dismissively. "But there are far more women than men in church these days."

"Are *you* ever one of them?" Emma asked, seizing the opportunity.

"I don't have time for church anymore - the weekends are so busy."

"I'd like to go to church," Tilly piped up unexpectedly. "One of my best friends, Bea, goes and she says there are lots of good stories from the Bible and they do colouring and sticking and everything. It sounds like fun."

"Perhaps you could ask if you might go with Bea sometime," Emma suggested.

"Could I, Mummy?" Tilly asked eagerly.

"I'm not very keen on Bea or her family," Rachel said disdainfully. "I don't know why the school has this policy of allowing a few children in on a full scholarship. It brings in all sorts of lower class youngsters, who are plainly out of their depth."

"I like Bea," Tilly replied staunchly. "She's kind. I'd like to go to her church sometime."

"We'll have to speak to Daddy," her mother temporised, plainly hoping that the question would be quickly forgotten; but once Harry had arrived and they were all sitting round the table later, tucking into Emma's carefully planned meal with every evidence of enjoyment, Tilly took advantage of a pause in the adults' conversation and said: "Daddy, could

I go to church with Bea sometime? Mummy says I have to ask you first but I'd really like to go because Bea says it's lots of fun."

Harry did not answer immediately but he looked at his older daughter frowningly and Rachel hastened to say that it was just a suggestion and that there was no need to think about it now as they would be away for the next sixteen days.

"Mmm," Harry replied absently. After another pause, he added, "It's a funny coincidence. I just learnt today that my boss goes to church – and our CEO is apparently a committed Christian, who is on his church leadership team and sometimes preaches. In fact, I've been invited by my boss to some big event in the City in the early autumn, where the CEO is speaking about how his faith shapes his life. I think I'll have to go – I don't want to upset my boss. I mean, he said it was entirely up to me – no pressure – but that's not how these things work, is it?"

"I would take him at face value," Emma replied. "But go anyway – you might find it gives you an interesting insight into your CEO's worldview and approach to life."

"So, can I go to church sometime with Bea?" Tilly persisted, not understanding much of the conversation.

"I expect so," her father replied impatiently. "Eat up and don't chatter. We'll need to be on our way soon."

Emma took this as a hint and began to clear away the main course. By the time she had served everyone with dessert, Millie and Joel were tired of their highchairs. They had enjoyed eating their fill of avocado and banana slices and throwing their toys on the floor for their cousins to retrieve but now they wanted a change of scenery. Knowing that their complaints would exasperate her brother-in-law,

Emma lifted them out one at a time and then sat with them on her lap, watching the others finish their desserts and listening while they talked excitedly about their holiday plans.

Seeing that she had her hands full, Rachel asked, albeit rather perfunctorily, whether her sister could manage, but she barely waited for Emma's assurance before continuing with her previous topic of conversation as she tucked into her slice of lemon torte.

When everyone had eaten their fill of dessert, except for Emma who had not had a hand free to wield a spoon, Harry began to issue abrupt orders intended to expedite the process of ensuring that each of his offspring had collected any belongings and made use of the facilities, repeatedly checking his watch and irritably adjuring everyone to 'get a move on.' In the midst of this bustle of noise and activity, his mobile phone rang and, on checking who was calling, Harry announced that it was an important client and he would have to take the call. Suddenly, the pressing need for haste was set aside as he prioritised his client's demands.

Emma did not feel qualified to question his decision to speak to his client but she did feel that his instant willingness to abandon his previous insistence on speed rather suggested that his initial attitude had been unnecessarily extreme.

She eventually waved her sister and family off on the first leg of their trip to Florida with a sigh of relief and was able to turn her attention to the customary bath and bedtime routine which would encourage the twins to settle for the night without protest.

CHAPTER 19

In retrospect, wry amusement was Emma's chief emotion as she reviewed her sister's visit. She had made all sorts of elaborate plans for speaking to her sister about her faith but in the end had barely created an opening to probe at all; meanwhile, the Lord was finding other ways to tackle the problem and was targeting Tilly and Harry in a two-pronged approach. To invite Tilly's interest by way of her friend was especially appropriate; to seek a response from Harry through more senior work colleagues was tactically brilliant; for the two lines of attack to coincide might turn out to be a masterstroke. Emma prayed that it would prove to be the case. Not only was Harry ambitious, but he was also hierarchically minded; if he thought it might be beneficial to humour his boss or there was any chance that he could catch the attention of his CEO, he might attend the meeting he had mentioned; and knowing that men more senior than him took Christianity seriously might encourage him to consider its claims more thoroughly than he had ever allowed himself to do in the past.

As for her sister's interference in her life, she would not give it another moment's thought. She was not about to start dolling herself up to go out looking for a husband. She supposed that there was some truth in the notion that the twins would be better off with a father as well as a mother – and sooner rather than later, but only if it were the right kind of father.

She felt uncomfortable at even touching in her thoughts on the possibility of putting another man in Sam's place as her husband and as a father to his children. She wondered guiltily what Sam would think of her. And then it occurred to her that he was with the Lord and that his outlook might be rather changed now. For the first time, she allowed herself to reflect that such considerations must be different when viewed from the perspective of heaven. Sam had been a good man - a kind man and a doting father; he would not expect his widow to struggle through the rest of her life alone if support and companionship offered; he would give an enthusiastic and positive assent to anything that would benefit Millie and Joel, anyone who could enhance their childhood and assist in launching them into adulthood.

Emma felt as though a weight had been lifted from her shoulders at this realisation. Subconsciously she had allowed herself to fall into the assumption that to honour Sam's memory meant to stay faithful, to keep herself set apart, alone. Now she saw that was a false position: Sam – like the Lord – would want her to live life in all its fullness, whatever that would mean for her. She would trust that God had a good plan for her life and for the twins, a plan to prosper them and not to harm them, a plan to give them hope and a future. Perhaps the Lord could even salvage the missed opportunity to understand Nick better so that she could somehow begin to look to the future rather than spending so much time reflecting on the past.

When Charlie called round with little Dan the following day, she commented on Emma's better spirits.

"There have been a number of developments," Emma replied tantalisingly.

"Tell me," Charlie invited.

"First, you tell me how you're feeling – and whether there's been any news at Ed's work."

"I'm okay. I think I'm getting over the worst of the morning sickness. Nothing more has been said to Ed about the work situation. Now, what are these developments?" Charlie asked, plainly eager to hear more.

While Dan investigated the contents of the toy box in the sitting room and the twins lay on the rug and Joel made unavailing attempts to crawl, Emma described her encounters with Milo and Fred in entertaining detail, explaining her relief over the fact that Fred had supplanted her as the object of Theresa's attentions, and reporting the commitment she had made to take Fred to church on Sunday.

"Is that why you're more cheerful?" Charlie asked, sounding puzzled and almost disappointed.

"I also had a visit from my sister and her family yesterday."

"She doesn't usually cheer you up."

"I'm not sure she meant to on this occasion, but she gave me some amusing sisterly advice."

Charlie snorted disrespectfully. "Such as?"

"Oh, she rather thinks I've let myself go, and apparently I'll need to make some changes if I want to – er – attract another man."

"She's always frighteningly smart and elegant, of course,

but you look lovely. You always do. What on earth would she say about *me*?"

Emma did not enlighten her friend.

"Anyway, *do* you?"

"Do I what?"

"Want to attract another man?"

"I'm not sure," Emma replied evasively. "It *has* occasionally crossed my mind since Sam died to wonder – theoretically – whether there might ever be someone else, but the idea made me feel so guilty that I pushed it aside. Then Rachel came along with her 'helpful' advice and, when I was thinking it through yesterday evening, it occurred to me that Sam would want us to be happy. It's such a relief to have straightened out my thoughts on that, so I'm really grateful to my sister – although I'm not sure that's what she intended. *Plus* – and you'll appreciate this – I had planned to try and talk to Rachel about her faith, but I made very little progress, and then Tilly asked whether she could go to church sometime with her friend and, in reply, Harry mentioned that his boss has invited him to some Christian meeting in the autumn. I'm pretty sure he'll go, because he won't want to upset his boss, so I've had to acknowledge that the Lord's plans are very much better than mine!"

Charlie was amused.

"Speaking of plans," she said after a moment, "Ed has got an interview at Nick's company on Friday week."

"That's great," Emma replied delightedly.

After a brief hesitation, Charlie commented, sounding slightly defensive, "Ed and I have decided that Nick is one of the good guys."

"How d'you work that out?"

"I know you don't trust him but, except for the way he treated you all those years ago, he seems to behave with a great deal of thoughtfulness and - and integrity."

"It's quite a big exception. Is there any good reason to overlook the way he treated me?" Emma asked hopefully.

"I think Ed knows more than I do, but you should probably ask Nick that. You must know he still likes you or he wouldn't have come over to give you a hand now and then. So far as Ed knows, he's not had any other girlfriends since he – well, since you."

"To be honest, Charlie, I just don't understand it – I don't understand *him*," Emma confessed. "Unless there's some kind of explanation for what happened six years ago, I've got no idea whether he – whether I could trust him."

"If it helps, Ed has said that he doesn't think Nick's had an easy time over the years. He's never told me anything more than that but I suppose he doesn't want to betray a confidence, particularly as you and I are friends and something might get back that wasn't meant to be passed on."

"I guess I'm just going to have to leave it with the Lord for now."

"And as you said a few minutes ago, the Lord's plans are better than ours," Charlie reminded her. "It's funny, isn't it, that when things get tough, we seem to learn so much more about our faith, and the Lord becomes so much more important – closer to us."

"If we let him," Emma agreed. "In fact, I was only reading this morning that passage in James where it says: 'Come near to God and he will come near to you.' It goes on to say that we should humble ourselves before the Lord and he will lift us up, and I was thinking that maybe that links to the quote I've put up on my fridge, which I've found really helpful: '*Trust in the Lord with all your heart and lean not on your own understanding; in all your ways acknowledge him, and he will make your paths straight.*' I'm not quite sure what 'in all your ways acknowledge him' means in practice but it must include humility before God and dependence on Him, so that we're seeking to be mindful of Him at all times and to discern His will in order to obey it."

"Yes," her friend agreed. "Although I find it very hard to discern His will. I just pray and muddle through, hoping the Lord will stop me if I'm barking up entirely the wrong tree."

"Most of us are a bit like that. When doors open or shut, I suppose we have to see God's hand in it. As Luke said recently, it's often only when we look back later that we can see that God was at work."

Having spread the entire contents of the toy box across the floor, Dan was beginning to lose interest in playthings that were intended for much younger children, so Emma and Charlie took him and the twins through to the kitchen for refreshments.

Nothing more was said about Nick, but the conversation had given Emma further food for thought and she chewed it over a great deal in the following days. She did not find any sudden inspiration or reach any new conclusions but she became steadily more convinced that she should have let Nick explain himself when he asked, instead of repulsing him. At times, she thought there could be no possible explanation which would satisfy her but, at others, she considered Ed and Penny's cryptic remarks and felt sure that there was some impenetrable mystery and that there was a great deal of good in Nick, as Charlie had asserted.

She was glad to be distracted from the unresolvable confusion of her thoughts by Joel's swift progress in the matter of crawling. Fortunately, he took a few days to master the art fully and Emma had time to baby-proof her house. Millie watched her brother with interest but did not seem to feel any pressing need to emulate his achievement and Emma was more inclined to be grateful that there was only one baby on the move for the time being than to worry about whether Millie was a little backward, particularly once she had looked the topic up in her baby-care manual and read that most babies begin to crawl between the ages of seven and ten months. It seemed that Joel was unusually active rather than Millie being unduly passive.

Joel's enthusiasm for his new-found ability to influence his location led him to object rather more strenuously at times to attempts to pin him down in his highchair, car seat or pushchair.

On Sunday morning he took great exception to being buckled into the car for the trip to church and Emma momentarily questioned the wisdom of her commitment to Fred and Theresa. Fortunately, he forgot his protests once they were underway and, although Fred's house was not very far away, he was in a perfectly good humour by the time they pulled on to the drive at thirty-two Wallace Road.

Theresa had plainly been watching for her arrival, for she came to the front door at once and, as Emma stepped out of the car, she called out, "Hello, dear. Could you come and give me a hand?"

"I can't leave the twins for long," Emma warned her.

"Oh, that's alright. I only want to give you Fred's medicine bag and his cushion. I've shut Milo and Barley in the kitchen already, so we just need to get Fred out to the car."

Emma took the items which Theresa passed to her, loaded them into the car and went back to the front door to see whether further help was needed.

Looking into the dark, shabby hallway, Emma was aware of the distinctive, musty odour of old age and unwashed dog. The décor was unmistakeably old-fashioned. Emma supposed it was almost inevitable that when you reached a sufficient age and your senses were less acute than they had once been, you would no longer notice or have the energy to care about the dilapidation of everything around you. If Fred's eyesight had deteriorated, it was likely that he couldn't see clearly enough to distinguish the details of his surroundings.

"Can I help at all?" she called, but Theresa emerged from a side door into the hall just at that moment, slowly escorting Fred, who had clearly dressed for church with great care. Despite its being almost the middle of August, he was wearing a shirt, tie, three-piece suit, smart shoes polished to a gloss, tweed trilby hat and buff raincoat, although he had left his coat unbuttoned, presumably as a concession to the season.

He apologised to Emma several times for his lack of speed and for his stiffness, which made settling him in the car a protracted manoeuvre. He also thanked her repeatedly for her assistance.

She fastened the seatbelt for him, becoming aware of the inimitable aroma of Old Spice in the confines of the car, and once Theresa had squeezed herself past Millie's car seat and established herself in the centre of the back seat of the car, they were able to set off.

"This is very good of you," Fred said for the umpteenth time, with charming courtesy.

They had to repeat the manoeuvre in reverse once they arrived at church and Emma thought Fred very stoic in bearing all the discomfort of the unaccustomed effort. He seemed to have significantly increased in infirmity in the short time she had known him. However, he plainly derived much satisfaction from the church service and from being treated with great care and attention by the stewards and the vicar. He explained to Michael after the service that he had formerly attended the local Methodist church with his wife, but had stopped when his wife fell ill and had somehow never got round to going again after she had passed away. "My loss," he acknowledged regretfully. "But I'm glad to have this opportunity to be here today; it is better to do something positive than to perpetuate past mistakes. Theresa, who has been quite wonderful, encouraged me to come with her and young Emma collected us. Everyone has been so kind."

Theresa enjoyed the praise but was soon reminding Fred that his next dose of medication was due imminently. While she extracted several pills and a bottle of water from his bag, one of the stewards hastened away to fetch a couple of cups of tea and a plate of shortbread fingers. Theresa stood over Fred while he swallowed his medicines, but then graciously allowed the steward to proffer the refreshments which Fred accepted with his usual gentle gratitude, saying politely that shortbread had always been a great favourite of his. He then engaged the steward in a conversation about his family and, by the time Emma had returned from collecting Millie and Joel from the crèche, he was sharing reminiscences about childhood and the many changes to the town over the years.

So polished were his manners and such was his air of immaculately groomed frailty that he had a considerable escort to attend him back to the car afterwards. As Emma pulled away, he waved to his new friends and well-wishers in a jaunty fashion but when she pulled on to his front drive he struggled to get out of the car and was plainly very much exhausted. His progress from the car to the house was painfully slow. Theresa led him unhurriedly over the paving stones to his front door and Emma hovered on his other side, anxious lest his tottering steps should falter and he should lose his footing.

Only when he was safely inside, did Emma return to the car for his cushion and bag. She carried them to the house, but as there was no sign of the others, she ventured into the gloomy hall and, following the sound of Theresa's voice, which could just be heard in the lulls between outbursts of enthusiastic barking from the dogs still shut in the kitchen, she tapped on the backroom door.

"Come in," Theresa called commandingly. "Oh, thank you, dear," she added when she saw what Emma was carrying. "Leave the bag on the table and put the cushion on Fred's chair – the green one in the corner. I'll just get Fred settled comfortably and then I'll see to Barley and Milo."

"Can I help at all?" Emma asked.

"No, no," Theresa declined categorically. "You get on home with the twins. I'll manage here."

"Well, if you're sure?"

"Yes, dear. Off you go!"

CHAPTER 20

Luke was due to arrive the following Friday and Emma was greatly looking forward to his visit, although she warned herself that he would probably want to spend a good proportion of the time with his girlfriend, assuming that the relationship was still working out for them both. As she began to plan out the weekend, with its several variables, it occurred to her that she ought to find out whether Fred would like to go to church again the following Sunday.

She phoned Theresa on Tuesday to enquire but there was no reply and no answerphone, so she left it until later in the day and called again. This time Theresa eventually answered, but when Emma explained the reason for her call, she said bluntly, "Oh no, dear! Fred has been very poorly today. I'm quite worried about him. I've been there most of the day but he's got no energy and very little appetite. I don't think we should try and get him to church next Sunday - I'm wondering whether taking him out was just too much for him."

"I'm sorry to hear he's not well. Is there anything I can do to help? Does he need any shopping?"

"I'm not sure how he'll cope tomorrow. I have to go and help my daughter, so I can't check on him till the evening.

Could you call round at some point during the day and see how he's doing?"

Emma agreed and paid her visit the following morning before going on to meet up with Charlie and Dan for lunch. Fred was very slow to open the front door and shuffled back to his chair afterwards with alarming unsteadiness and effortful breathing. He was as courteous as ever but definitely subdued. There was no sign of Milo, and Fred explained that Theresa had taken him with her the previous evening so that she could give him some exercise. She intended to return him at the end of the day.

Grateful not to have to fend off an over-excited terrier, Emma brought the twins inside in their car seats so that she could make Fred a cup of tea. She was able to persuade him to eat a digestive biscuit with his drink, as it seemed that he had had very little breakfast, but he would not take another biscuit. He said that it all seemed to be too much effort. On reflection, she decided that she should prepare him a quick meal before she left. She texted Charlie to warn her that she would be a little delayed, then hunted around to see what food was available.

The state of the kitchen was rather daunting but she tried not to look too closely at the quantity of crumbs and dirt collected at the bottom of the cutlery drawer and made no attempt to investigate the recesses of his cupboards. She hoped his constitution was accustomed to the lack of hygiene and could only be grateful that she would not be sharing his meal. Having located some eggs and other basic supplies, she made him scrambled egg on toast and served it to him on a lap tray so that he could stay in his comfortable chair. He was touchingly grateful, and even more so when she promised to drop in again later to clear up. She hoped his gratitude and his good manners would prompt him to finish the meal and left him with the television on for company.

Describing some of this to Charlie over lunch in a local café, she found that her friend was rather shocked at her involvement in caring for such an elderly gentleman.

"I've been thinking about it on and off since you first told me you were taking him to church and, to be honest, I think you've got more than enough on your plate," she told Emma bluntly. "Theresa should have asked someone else. She's a tiresome woman!"

"It's only because I live nearby," Emma said. "I don't mind helping now and then. I don't suppose it'll amount to much. Theresa won't want to relinquish too much control. She loves to be needed."

"If she keeps trying to involve you, let me know and I'll give you a hand."

"Some people might think you've got plenty on your plate too," Emma pointed out, and Charlie acknowledged the hit with a smile and a grimace, as she offered Millie a spoonful of pureed carrot.

The twins were occupying the café's only two highchairs, and Emma and Charlie were taking turns at feeding them, in between snatching mouthfuls of their own lunch, while Dan sat on a proper chair with a booster seat and worked his way steadily through a plate of beans and chips.

His serious concentration on the matter in hand reminded Emma of his father.

"How is Ed feeling about his interview on Friday?" she enquired.

"Okay. We've been asking God to overrule in all this,

and Ed seems quite relaxed at the moment. If he doesn't get the job, he'll know it wasn't where God wanted him to be just now. He's seeing Nick after work this evening and they'll chat through anything it might be useful for him to know before the interview, so he'll have done all he can to improve his chances."

"Give him my best wishes," Emma remarked.

"Nick?" Charlie asked provocatively.

"*No!*" Emma repudiated the suggestion with considerable force, even though she knew that Charlie was perfectly well aware that she had meant Ed.

Her friend giggled but forbore to tease her any further.

"I still don't like the idea of you getting involved in looking after Fred when you've already got your hands full with Millie and Joel to care for," Charlie said a little later.

"Actually, Luke is coming to stay this weekend so I'll have company and some help for a few days."

"Good! You could definitely do with some help. You look too delicate."

"My sister told me I'd lost too much weight - but I do try and eat sensibly."

"You just don't have time to look after yourself: twins are hard work. Sometimes you look worn out – and so sad. I really feel for you."

"The loneliness is difficult," Emma acknowledged. "It's silly, because the twins are always around, so I'm not alone; but they're not yet great conversationalists! Anyway, don't let me complain. I have a great friend who invites me out to lunch now and then and keeps me company when I'm down."

"You do?" Charlie was mystified.

"Yes – *you,* silly! You've been so good, keeping an eye on me. With all the church midweek activities stopped for the summer, you're my main, adult contact."

"Has Nick called round lately?"

"No," Emma replied bleakly. She thought of Nick as she had seen him last, when she had refused to listen to him and had rebuffed him so completely. If only she had been less uncompromising, there might have been some possibility of renewing communication, but as it was she had burnt her boats. She wondered how he was doing and almost asked Charlie whether she knew anything, but stopped herself. It was better not to dwell on such thoughts.

"That's strange," Charlie commented, but anything else she might have said was lost as Joel demanded some attention and Dan dropped his fork.

Joel was quickly appeased with some toys from Emma's bag and Dan was soon supplied with a clean fork, but Emma worked hard to keep the conversation on other topics and lunch was finished without any further reference to Nick.

Emma did not disclose to her friend that she intended to call on Fred again on the way home, as she rather thought that Charlie might insist on accompanying her. The twins fell asleep en route, so it was easy enough for Emma to pop in, clear up his lunch tray and make sure he was comfortable, but she did not feel that she could linger and, as she left, she could not help thinking that Fred looked forlorn and far from well. She supposed that he might be missing the companionship of his little dog and hoped that Theresa's return later in the day would lift his spirits.

Theresa took the trouble to call Emma during the course of the evening and let her know that she had checked in on Fred and found that all was well. She thanked Emma for her efforts in a graciously dismissive way that grated a little but, on the whole, Emma was impressed by Theresa's indefatigable concern for Fred and Milo and could only be grateful to God that her tendency to officious interference had found the perfect outlet.

On Friday morning, Emma woke early and spent a while in prayer. She thought again of Fred and Theresa and lifted them before the Lord. She did not forget that it was the day of Ed's interview and she prayed for the right outcome for him. She also offered up rather less well-formulated prayers for her own situation and for her ongoing desire to be trusting in the Lord and honouring him in every area of her life, as well as for making the most of Luke's visit and unresentfully promoting opportunities for him to see his girlfriend.

Luke was due to arrive late in the evening and Emma took time to phone Charlie as soon as she had got the twins to bed, to enquire after Ed. According to Charlie, he felt the interview had gone well; another bonus was that he had been told he would hear either way within a week, so he would not be kept for long on tenterhooks. Emma charged her friend to tell her as soon as there was any news and rang off, wondering what to do with her evening. She did not normally have a problem filling her time but the anticipation of Luke's visit was somehow unsettling. She was entirely ready for his arrival but could not seem to summon up the willpower to set her mind to anything else. In the end, she fetched some mending and sat with the television on in the background while she stitched up the hem of a skirt and darned several pairs of socks.

Her brother laughed at her when he arrived, saying that he didn't know anyone who bothered to mend socks any more.

"I don't like to waste them if they can be easily fixed."

"If that's your yardstick, I'm safe. I'd never find it easy to mend anything!"

They stayed up chatting late into the night but Luke was up again bright and early on Saturday morning to help his sister with the twins. When Emma teased him on missing out on a lie-in, he replied that, if she could manage to keep going, he had no possible excuse for laziness. "Plus, I have a confession to make. I'm heading into London again later so I want to make the most of the morning with my nephew and niece."

"Are you seeing your girlfriend?" Emma asked, determined not to sound disappointed.

He nodded. "So what would you most like to do with the morning?" he enquired. "Your wish is my command!"

"Let's go up to the local nursery. I'd like to get a few plants for the garden and I'm told they have a pet store and an aquarium section that are good for looking round with little ones."

Luke was perfectly amenable and they spent a couple of pleasant hours browsing all that was on offer and enjoying Millie and Joel's fascination with the small, furry animals in various enclosures and the colourful, shimmering fish in the serried rows of tanks.

When the time came to leave the garden centre, Luke insisted on paying for Emma's purchases. Unloading the car at home, he referred to it his 'guilt offering', although Emma told him not to be silly. "I understand that you've only got a few days in the UK and that you'll want to see your girlfriend," she said. "I wish you'd tell me more about her," she added. "I don't even know her name."

"I'd like to invite her for lunch tomorrow," he replied. "Would that work?"

"Invite her *here*?"

"Yes. But if it's a problem, I'll take us all out somewhere."

"No, it'll be fine. I was just wondering what I could cook. I'll defrost some chicken pieces overnight and do a casserole. It'll be lovely to meet her."

"Can we still get to church in the morning?"

"Yes. I'll leave the casserole on a low heat while we're out."

"What time will we be home?"

"About half past eleven."

"Great."

"So now you *have* to tell me about her," Emma said.

"You've met her," he grinned.

"No, I haven't," Emma denied, puzzled. "You've been very secretive."

"Yes - but you've met her. It's Penny Knight."

There was a stunned silence.

"*Nick's* sister?" Emma asked eventually, trying to digest all the implications.

Luke nodded, grinning again at her amazement. "I met her after Sam's service of thanksgiving and we kept in touch."

"Well, you might have told me!"

"I have."

"Yes, but I mean – *before!* Although, now I come to think of it, you did say you'd been talking to a very pretty girl. Presumably that was Penny?"

"Yep!"

"Does Nick know?"

"Penny told him after my last visit, but I haven't met him yet. Penny's planning to introduce us this afternoon. Shall I ask him to join us for lunch tomorrow?"

Emma's pulse beat faster but she could not tell whether it was from anticipation or dread. "I don't suppose he'll want to come," she remarked after a moment, trying not to sound wistful.

"Penny hasn't divulged much," her brother said kindly. "I understood that there was something between you and Nick, but perhaps you'd better tell me what's been happening."

"It's complicated."

"Tell me over lunch," Luke suggested.

CHAPTER 21

Once a big bowl of couscous salad had been set on the kitchen table and the twins had been loaded into their high chairs and supplied with their own food, Luke commanded his sister to 'spill the beans.'

Emma thought for a moment and then hesitantly began. "Nick's been round a few times recently to help with the garden – and with other jobs – he fixed that dripping tap in the bathroom for me, which was very kind. But a - a few weeks ago I told him I didn't want to see him again."

"Did you mean it?"

"I don't know."

"*Don't know!*" Luke echoed incredulously, pausing in the act of spooning couscous on to his plate.

"I - I meant it at the time. After all, Sam only died four months ago. I felt guilty even thinking about the possibility that there might ever be someone else – and – and other people would think it was indecent."

"Is it?"

"No! But I was – I *am* confused," Emma admitted miserably.

"You can't worry about what people think. You need to decide what's right for you and the twins."

"*You* don't think it would be wrong with Sam gone so recently?"

"He *is* gone. He wouldn't begrudge you any happiness."

"I've thought that too but I'm not convinced I would be happy."

"With Nick?"

"Yes."

"Then why are we having this discussion?" Luke asked, pardonably exasperated.

"The problem is that I can't trust him," Emma explained pursuing her own thoughts.

"Why not?"

"Because of what he did six years ago."

"Now you've lost me," Luke remarked, shaking his head. "What did he do six years ago?"

"Don't you remember? He dumped me with a text message and just walked away."

"Oh, he's *that* chap!"

"There haven't been any others. But how can I trust someone who treated me so badly?"

"It's a long time ago. Perhaps he's changed – or perhaps he had a reason."

"Afterwards, I racked my brains to try and work out what I might have said or done to upset him, but I couldn't think of anything."

"I didn't imagine it was anything *you'd* done, but he must have had a reason," Luke said firmly. "No one behaves that nastily without justification – real or imagined."

"What justification could there be for acting like that?"

"I don't know. Maybe he's like Mr Rochester and he's got a mad wife hidden away somewhere."

"Don't be ridiculous," Emma smiled reluctantly.

"Have you ever asked him?"

"Whether he's got a mad wife?"

"For an explanation."

"Of course! When he texted me to say he couldn't see me anymore, I replied immediately asking why. Then I phoned a couple of times but only got his answerphone. I left messages, but he never replied. It was – crushing. In the end, I gave up. He'd cut off all communication and I decided I had to stop - stop grovelling."

"It makes no sense. People don't behave like that. You have to ask him what he thought he was doing."

"It's too embarrassing."

"It sounds as though there's too much at stake to let that stop you."

"But it's difficult – he asked for an opportunity to explain and I wouldn't listen."

"When?"

"A few weeks ago – when I told him not to come round anymore."

Luke exhaled deeply.

"I'm sorry," Emma said wretchedly. "I told you it was complicated."

"Yes. You did warn me!" He lapsed into reflection, finishing off the last few mouthfuls of his lunch absent-mindedly, but a few minutes later he laid down his knife and fork and said decisively, "We should definitely have Nick round with Penny tomorrow and try to clear the air. I'll speak to him this afternoon."

"Oh, but –" Emma began.

"This has got to be sorted," Luke interrupted ruthlessly.

"It'll be easier while Penny and I are around, so let's invite him and see what he says."

Emma did not try to argue any further. Although it was going to be very awkward to sit down to lunch with Nick after their last encounter, she had longed for the opportunity to ask him for an explanation and it would be foolish to refuse it now simply on the grounds of embarrassment. She also remembered Fred's comment: 'it is better to do something positive than to perpetuate past mistakes.'

She waved her brother off for his meeting with Penny and Nick with some trepidation, praying that this latest development would prove to be a helpful one and that, whatever the outcome, her difficulties with Nick would not have a detrimental impact on Luke's relationship with Penny. She suspected that Luke's eagerness to resolve the situation might be as much attributable to his concern for Penny as to his affection for his sister and allowed that it was only right and proper that he should be eager to promote Penny's happiness.

Later that evening, Luke was able to report to Emma with evident satisfaction that, with a little persuasion from his sister, Nick had agreed to accompany her to lunch the following day.

"He wasn't easy to convince," Luke admitted. "He was so sure you couldn't really want to include him in the invitation that Penny resorted to suggesting that you might think it had become important to find a way to get along with him now you've learnt that your brother is seeing his sister."

"That's true, of course," Emma agreed reflectively. "Although I hadn't thought of it."

"So defrost an extra chicken piece or two," Luke told her cheerily. "Penny's going get Nick over here shortly after eleven thirty and then she and I will take Millie and Joel out and give you some space to have your chat with Nick."

"It seems a bit contrived."

"It is, but don't worry about it. You need answers. Then maybe you can decide whether to trust him."

"If we're going to get to church tomorrow morning, I'd better do more than just defrost the chicken this evening," Emma remarked.

Luke offered to help, but warned his sister that he was not particularly domesticated and that if she expected him to do anything more than peel a few potatoes, she would be sadly disappointed. Accordingly, she handed him the bag of potatoes while she herself set to work to chop the onions, make the stock and gather together the ingredients and equipment needed for the casserole.

"So tell me all about Penny," Emma commanded as they worked side by side.

"Not much to tell. I liked her as soon as I saw her."

"She *is* lovely," Emma agreed.

"Sweet-natured too," Luke went on. "And very fond of her brother."

Emma agreed again.

"In fact, she's fond of all her family," Luke continued. "And, as you will know, it's a big family. One of the reasons I'm in England this time round is to look at the possibility of moving back to London. I don't think Penny would be happy coming out to Singapore."

"You're serious then?"

"*I* am. I hope Penny is too. I should hear on Monday

whether there's a place for me in the London office. If not, I'll start looking around."

"You'd move to a different company?"

"Yes."

"You *are* serious!" Emma remarked in surprise. "I never thought you'd leave – you're doing so well where you are."

"I'm optimistic that they'll let me transfer to London."

"Have you told Penny all this?"

"She knows I'm hoping to move back here."

"I'll pray about it," Emma offered.

"I'll pray for you and Nick," her brother returned. "In fact, why don't we pray now?"

So they sat at the kitchen table and prayed for one another and, although it felt slightly embarrassing and unfamiliar, it was a great encouragement to be able share and support one another in this way and both agreed afterwards that they should do it more often.

CHAPTER 22

Emma did not sleep well that night. Her thoughts kept jumping ahead to the anticipated encounter with Nick and, although she could not begin to guess how the meeting would unfold, she nevertheless envisaged all kinds of improbable scenarios and rehearsed various speeches of challenge and reproach.

She was also rather distracted during the Sunday morning service and several times had to recall her wandering thoughts and apologise silently to the Lord for her inattention.

As the time for Nick's arrival drew closer, Emma began to think she had been crazy to agree to this meeting. How could she face him with all that lay between them and after her vehement refusal to listen to him? How could he possibly have any satisfactory explanation for the past? And, if it was horribly embarrassing, how could they sit down together to a meal afterwards and behave as if nothing was wrong? It would be insupportable. She reminded herself that, in bearing what was thought to be unbearable, the human spirit often proved stronger than anticipated and, as she could see no way out of the meeting, she tried to resign herself to the inevitable.

Returning from church, Emma found herself very much

on edge, listening for sounds of their guests' arrival. When the doorbell finally rang shortly after half-past eleven, Emma was tempted to hide in the kitchen and let Luke answer it by himself, but she did not wish to appear unwelcoming towards Penny, so she followed her brother out into the hall and hovered shyly behind him.

While Luke and Penny greeted one another, Emma glanced cautiously beyond them to see that Nick was also hanging back and had remained standing on the doorstep as if he doubted whether he should enter. His expression was reserved and, when Emma's gaze met his, there was a hint of a question in his look. She gave him an awkward half smile, which was sufficient to bring him over the threshold, and, as he turned to close the door, she invited everyone to come through to the kitchen, leading the way rather self-consciously.

The twins had been temporarily installed in their playpen and, once Penny had handed over to Emma the bunch of lilies and carnations she had been carrying, she made her way straight over to them, crouching down to say a cheerful hello, but Nick still hung back, looking uncomfortable. Luke took charge of proceedings, offered the visitors refreshments and engaged Nick in conversation, leaving Emma free to speak to Penny and to smile over their previous meeting.

"I wanted to tell you that I was seeing Luke," Penny confessed. "But it was all rather difficult."

"I know," Emma agreed fervently.

"Thank you for inviting Nick over," Penny added shyly. She looked as though she would have liked to say something more but, as she hesitated, Luke came over with a cup of coffee for her and the talk became more general.

Emma did not contribute much to the conversation. Most of her mind was preoccupied with a growing dread over her impending discussion with Nick and she was aware too of her position as hostess and her responsibilities for providing the meal. She thought that Nick was also rather quiet and she conceded that their projected discussion was unlikely to be easy for him either. She began to wish that they could just get on with it: the sooner they started, the sooner it would all be over. However, when Luke put down his empty cup and suggested that it was time to load his niece and nephew into the pushchair, her heart seemed to leap into her throat and she thought she would do almost anything to postpone the inevitable for a little longer.

Whether or not Luke sensed his sister's panic, he pressed calmly on. "We'll head for the park. The weather's good, so we'll take our time – unless these little rascals yell. We'll be straight back if they're noisy."

Emma lifted Joel out of the playpen and carried him to the pushchair; Luke followed suit with Millie. Once they were both safely strapped in, Luke held out a hand to Penny and together they manoeuvred the pushchair out of the room. Emma waved them off from the front door and returned reluctantly to the kitchen where Nick had remained throughout.

He was standing by the back door, gazing away down the garden, but he turned as she moved forwards and watched her silently as she went over to the oven, ostensibly to check on her casserole but, if truth be told, simply to delay the necessity of meeting his eyes and opening the discussion. She peeped needlessly at the potatoes before switching the hob on underneath the pan and adding a little salt, then she moved towards the fridge, thinking rather incoherently that she could find the green vegetables which were to accompany the meal; and all the while her heart was beating suffocatingly fast and her nerves were stretched almost to breaking point.

Just then, Nick cleared his throat and, taking a step away from the door, said evenly, "Thank you for allowing me to accompany Penny."

Emma span round to face him, pulses jumping, but could not meet his eyes.

"This isn't going to be easy for either of us," he went on carefully. "But as Luke and Penny seem to be serious about one another we'll have to meet occasionally. I – I understand that you don't like me much, but Penny and Luke think it might help if I – if we cleared the air."

Emma glanced up briefly. "Maybe," she conceded. "I have wondered," she added after a moment in a very small voice, "Could you tell me what went so wrong six years ago that you had to finish with me so – so suddenly?"

"I am hugely sorry for the hurt I caused then – I always was. I would be very glad to try and explain."

He paused and then walked over to the kitchen table, pulled out a chair and lowered himself on to it.

"Won't you sit down?" he invited, gesturing to a chair opposite. "This could take a while."

She hesitantly advanced and took the chair he had indicated and sat with her hands grasping the edge of the chair seat, gazing down at the table top, which was covered with a cheerful, yellow, chequered plastic cloth.

Nick seemed to gather his thoughts. When he began, he spoke steadily, as if he were recounting something he had rehearsed many times before.

"First, I'm going to go back to when I was eighteen. I know that sounds ridiculous, but bear with me. In my last year at school, I caught mumps. Mum is convinced I was vaccinated as a child but either she's mistaken or it was ineffective. Anyway, there were complications, but eventually I made what I thought was a full recovery. I don't know whether you know anything about the possible effects of mumps but, for men, one very rare consequence can be infertility."

Emma's hands went to her mouth in dismay. This was so unexpected, so far from what she had thought they would be discussing, and yet she began to have an inkling of where this might be heading.

"When I met you," Nick went on resolutely, "that episode of illness was more than six years in the past and I had given it very little thought since then. You know that I fell in love with you and, since it seemed – wonderfully – that you felt the same, I planned to spend the rest of my life with you. That was the happiest summer of my life. We spoke now and then of the future and I gathered that you took it for granted that you would have a family one day. At that point, it didn't cross my mind to think things through any further." He paused for a moment and then continued doggedly. "Perhaps you remember that you were on the crèche rota at your church in Bristol and that, on a couple of occasions, I gave you a hand there?"

She nodded dumbly.

"I saw that you were very good with the little ones."

"So were you," Emma interpolated.

Nick's mouth twisted wryly. "On the second occasion, I was watching you comfort a little baby and thinking fondly that you would make a great mother – and it struck me that I had never tried to find out whether the mumps had had any lasting consequences. I knew I would have to look into it – although, to be honest, I assumed that everything would be fine. You can probably guess that the test results were *not* fine. I was told that I couldn't ever expect to have children. That was a bitter blow. I suppose most young people imagine they'll have a family at some point - that's what their parents did, after all. Then, on top of that disappointment, I realised that, in the circumstances, I could not possibly expect you to be willing to marry me – to make that kind of sacrifice."

Emma's heart turned over with pain - with pity for him and for herself. *This* was the reason for all the anguish they had both suffered.

"I understand," she said compassionately, and with that statement she meant to convey to him that she understood everything – all that he had done and left undone, all that he had said and left unsaid, all that they had both endured.

"Yes," Nick acknowledged flatly, misunderstanding. "I knew you'd agree. Needless to say, I tried to find a way round the situation; I thought and prayed and pleaded with God; but however much I wanted to, I could not persuade myself that it would be right to ask you, when you were only twenty, to decide whether you could bear to forfeit the prospect of ever having a family - a decision which would affect the whole of the rest of your life – and so, as you know, I ended the relationship. It was the – *the* hardest thing I've ever done. And the heartache didn't end there - every text, every message you sent in response cut me to the quick. So many times I almost replied, almost gave in to the temptation to tell you everything."

"Oh, how I wish you had!" Emma exclaimed impulsively.

He stood up abruptly and paced hastily away towards the door to the garden and back again, and came to stand at one end of the table leaning on his hands, his gaze bent downwards and a lock of dark hair tumbling forward over his forehead.

"You don't mean that," he said heavily.

"I can't begin to explain to you the – the pain of not knowing why it was all over," she replied, her throat tight with unshed tears.

"I know," he said gently, glancing up at her and away again. "I knew that at the time – but I also knew that as soon as I explained you would be trapped."

"Trapped?"

"Yes, because once you knew the truth, how could you walk away?"

"I – I see."

"I reasoned it all through. You were too good – too sweet – to abandon me at such a time, however much you really wanted children of your own, so I couldn't allow you to find out the truth. *I* would have to be the one to walk away. I realised that you would be badly hurt but I told myself that you were young, you'd only known me for a few months, you would get over it and find someone else. I was desperate to see you again but I was afraid that, even if I didn't blurt out the truth, I would give myself away somehow, so I sent that text, even though everything in me was screaming at me to keep quiet."

Emma wanted to tell him that there was no need for him to say anything more, no need to relive all the detail of those harrowing days, but she sensed that he felt compelled to give a full account, that in confessing everything he might find some relief.

"I knew," he continued, "that a text was the worst possible way to end a relationship – cowardly and cruel – but at the time that seemed a point in its favour: if it made you think badly of me, perhaps you would recover sooner. That was also why I couldn't allow myself to reply to any of your messages – apart from the fact that there was nothing I could say anyway. It was horribly cruel, but I had a reason. I'm so sorry."

"It's alright. I understand now," Emma said softly and reached out to cover his left hand with hers. His explanation had changed everything; he was completely restored to her good opinion.

For a moment he stared at her slender hand covering his, then he pulled away sharply, turned and strode to the back door and stood staring down the garden, as if to put as much distance between himself and Emma as possible or as if he longed to escape. Emma could see how rigidly he held himself.

He spoke jerkily, running an impatient hand through his hair to brush it off his forehead while still staring unseeingly out of the window: "And I was right – you *did* recover, you *did* find someone else. And the fact that I – have never got over it is not your problem, it's mine; but now we must somehow find a way forward – for Penny and Luke's sake."

He must have heard her chair scrape on the floor as Emma stood up but he did not look round. She knew now what she had to do and she sent up an arrow prayer asking for the right words to say to him.

Nick continued with difficulty. "I – I must apologise for what happened last time I was here. It will not happen again."

Emma moved to stand behind him. "Not?" she asked softly.

She heard his sharp intake of breath and saw him brace himself before he turned slowly to face her.

"Emma!" he began protestingly, but she laid a hand on his arm and he stopped short.

She looked up at him tenderly and said simply, "Nick, I love you. I've *always* loved you."

It seemed at first as if he could not believe it, but then, very slowly, his expression changed and at last he pulled her into his arms and kissed her, holding her as though he could never bear to let her go.

Eventually, Emma remembered the dinner and, gently disengaging herself, hastened to check her cooking. The casserole was simmering gently and smelled delicious, but the potatoes were irredeemably soft.

"Oh dear. It all goes to show that you should never mix romance and cookery," Emma remarked, torn between happiness and dismay.

Nick grinned unrepentantly. "What can I do to help?"

"Mash the potatoes and pretend that was the plan all along," she suggested laughingly.

She found the necessary utensils, the butter, milk and seasonings, and passed them all to Nick, who went exuberantly to work and soon produced a creamy-looking mash. Emma, meanwhile, fetched the green vegetables from the fridge and began to chop the florets off a head of broccoli. Every so often they would glance at one another and smile, almost in disbelief and certainly in great joy.

"Do you realise," Emma asked, "that last Friday was the sixth anniversary of the day you sent that text? Six years almost to the day and here we are!"

"God is very good," Nick replied sincerely. "Although they've not been easy years - for either of us."

"Worse for you," she said. "I never thought I'd say that, but definitely worse for you."

"I don't think that can possibly be correct when I think of what you've been through, but there were certainly many times when I thought that it would have been better for both of us if we had never met. I had naively imagined that the pain would diminish with time but for me it did not. And if I'd not had my faith to sustain me it would have been even harder. As I said, I'd prayed about the situation at the time and I was certain that I'd made the right decision; and I held on to the promises in scripture and tried to live by them."

"Any particular promises?"

"Three that I kept coming back to. Romans Eight: '*And we know that in all things God works for the good of those who love him*,' Psalm Twenty-Seven '*I remain confident of this: I will see the goodness of the Lord in the land of the living. Wait for the Lord; be strong and take heart and wait for the Lord.*' and Proverbs Three: '*Trust in the Lord with all your heart and lean not on your own understanding; in all your ways acknowledge him, and he will make your paths straight.*' Those were especially helpful."

"Look at my fridge," Emma told him, smiling as she moved to the sink to fill a saucepan with water.

"Pardon?"

"Look at my fridge."

Puzzled, Nick complied and saw the quote from Proverbs written out in Emma's handwriting. "You've found it helpful too," he observed.

Emma nodded. "I've prayed that through a great deal recently," she said. "It's not easy to live it out day by day, but it does seem that even feeble attempts on our part to trust in the Lord and depend on him are blessed by him." As she turned the hob on to heat the water for the broccoli, she added rather more prosaically, "I hope Luke and Penny will be back soon. Otherwise, the dinner will be past its best."

"It's very kind of them to take the twins out," Nick remarked. "I like your brother, by the way."

"And I like your sister."

"I think you *will* like her, but you've barely met her."

"Did she tell you that she called round here one evening a couple of weeks ago?"

"No. Why did she do that?"

"To try to put things right for you."

Nick looked nonplussed. "What did she say?"

"Not a great deal. She must have thought I knew more than I did. She mentioned in passing that things had been difficult for you and referred to health problems, but that was all. I think she hoped to persuade me to get in touch with you and sort things out, but how could I? I had burnt my boats by sending you away with such finality. I- I am sorry I reacted so angrily that day. There were so many things I had – misunderstood."

"It was hardly your fault," Nick reassured her. "I was a fool. And I should have explained things sooner. I wanted to, but it was difficult to introduce the subject into general conversation and, in any event, I had told myself I should wait – give you time and space. I couldn't imagine the grief you must feel over Sam's loss nor begin to guess how long you might need before you could think of anything – anyone else – if, in fact, you ever could."

"We must talk about Sam sometime but perhaps not now, not yet."

"No problem," Nick said equably.

"The truth is that I never really stopped thinking about you at one level," Emma confessed. "I fell in love with you six years ago and I couldn't stop loving the man I had imagined you to be. When you told me you couldn't see me anymore – and in such a painful way! – I supposed that your real character must be very different from what I had thought. I was hurt and angry; but I was still in love with the ideal you'd shown me over that summer. That probably sounds as confused as my emotions were back then: does it make any sense at all?"

"I think so – although I expected you to hate me. I wasn't at all surprised that you were resentful when we met again in the spring."

"I hadn't imagined there could be any kind of explanation that would so completely vindicate you," Emma said apologetically.

"It's not the kind of thing anyone could guess. No wonder there were misunderstandings."

"Some of the misunderstandings were my fault," she admitted ruefully. "I'll explain later. But when we first met again at Charlie's house, I felt very uncomfortable – I felt I needed to keep you at a distance. I told myself I didn't trust you, but that was a rationalisation of a host of indefinable and unreasonable reactions."

"Everything about our dealings with one another has been extraordinary and complicated. It's hardly surprising that there's been some confusion."

Nick came over as he spoke and slipped an affectionate and encouraging arm round her waist, but as Emma turned gratefully towards him, he caught her against him and kissed her thoroughly.

They were interrupted by a splutter and a loud hiss as the saucepan boiled over. They fell apart, laughing, and Emma hastily turned off the gas and moved the saucepan to another hob.

Between them, Nick and Emma laid the table and were just putting the final items in place when Luke and Penny returned with their charges. Millie and Joel were impatient to be extracted from their pushchair and Emma thought they were probably hungry so she hastily warmed their milk and apple puree.

"It's easier to humour them," she explained. "Once they've been fed, they might let us eat our meal in relative peace."

Luke and Penny continued their good offices and took charge of a twin apiece, installed them in their highchairs and fed them as much of the puree as managed to make it into their mouths and did not end up on their bibs, the highchairs or around their faces. The twins then finished their milk with evident enjoyment, while Emma brought the dinner and the warm plates to the table. She deftly cleaned the twins up and Luke found them each a few toys to play with. Once they were settled, Emma invited Nick to say grace. He paused for a moment before thanking the Lord for food, family, friends, fellowship and forgiveness.

"So," Luke remarked, as the food was being served, "I take it you've resolved your differences?"

Emma and Nick's eyes met across the table and they smiled tenderly at one another.

"Okay. There's no need to answer that question," Luke observed with dry humour.

Nick grinned and Emma blushed.

"I'm so pleased!" Penny exclaimed delightedly. "It's what I've been praying for ever since Nick told me he'd met you again."

"While we were out walking, Penny put me more fully in the picture," Luke told Nick, as they all began to eat. "That was a tough decision you made, splitting up with Emma – a tough decision at a tough period of your life."

"Would you have done the same?" Nick asked, genuinely interested to hear his answer.

"I'd like to think so," Luke replied seriously. "But no one knows till they're faced with that kind of situation exactly how they'll react. I'm not sure my altruism would be equal to the challenge."

"It wasn't entirely altruistic. I was also concerned that, long-term, there could be great bitterness between us over the inability to have a family. I saw that kind of rift develop between friends of my parents; there were months of tears and recriminations and an eventual divorce. It was very sad and destructive."

"D'you mean Dawn and John?" Penny asked.

When Nick nodded, she added: "I never really knew why they broke up."

"It was rather complicated. When they met and married,

neither of them wanted children; but Dawn changed her mind when she got older. I think she was in her late thirties – perhaps she realised that time was running out. Anyway, she tried everything to persuade John but he was adamant that he'd never wanted a family and wasn't going to give in to pressure. Dawn was so desperate that, without telling him, she stopped taking the pill. After a while, she got pregnant and had to confess to him. He was furious at the deception and walked out, refusing to have anything more to do with her. A month or two later, she miscarried and lost the baby, but John still couldn't forgive her, so they were divorced."

"How tragic," Emma said, genuinely saddened by the tale.

There was a short pause, while everyone reflected pensively on what they had just heard, but Luke soon lightened the mood by pointing out that he was entitled to be very smug.

"How come?" Nick asked suspiciously.

"I *told* Emma you must have had a good reason for breaking up with her."

"Yes," Emma interpolated with amusement. "If I recall correctly, you suggested that Nick might have a mad wife tucked away somewhere, like Mr Rochester!"

"That would have been much more romantic," Nick conceded.

"W-rong but w-romantic!" Luke pointed out, laughing as he emphasised the start of each word.

Penny looked puzzled, but it seemed that Nick had also read '1066 And All That'. "Does that mean I'm 'right but repulsive'?" he asked light-heartedly.

"Well, you repelled Emma very effectively for six years!" Luke joked.

CHAPTER 23

By the time the meal had been cleared away, the twins were ready for their afternoon nap. Emma gathered a rather grumpy Millie up out of her highchair and Nick promptly picked Joel up and offered to carry him upstairs.

"Take your time," Luke said flippantly. "Don't mind us!"

Nick grinned cheerfully and followed Emma from the room.

They changed the babies side by side and settled them in their cots; Emma pulled the bedroom door gently closed and smiled warmly up at Nick. He opened his arms and she walked into his steady embrace; they stood silently for some moments on the landing, simply holding one another close. Nick tucked Emma's head under his chin and rested his cheek against her soft curls.

"I never imagined I would be this happy," he said quietly after a little while.

"Nor I."

There was another pause.

"I suppose we should go back down," Emma whispered eventually.

"In a minute," Nick replied, releasing his hold but only so that he could tilt her chin up with one hand and kiss her. They clung together.

When Nick finally lifted his lips from hers, he said shakily, "Emma, my darling, marry me! Please marry me!"

"Oh, yes!" she sighed blissfully and pulled his head down for another kiss.

They reappeared downstairs a few minutes later, entering the kitchen rather sheepishly but with attempted nonchalance. They need not have worried, however, for they found Luke and Penny occupied in a very similar fashion.

Luke released Penny unhurriedly and smiled tenderly at her blushes. "I've just asked Penny to marry me," he announced matter-of-factly. "And, in case you were wondering, she said yes!"

Nick and Emma looked at one another and started to laugh.

"I've just asked Emma to marry me," Nick revealed. "And, in case you were wondering, she said yes!"

General hilarity ensued, but was interrupted by a loud knock at the door.

Nick raised an eyebrow at Emma and they both moved to answer it, opening the front door to disclose Theresa Halton standing squarely on the doorstep, as was her habit. Emma had just sufficient time to note that she was sans bag and sans dog, before she spoke.

"Oh, *you're* here!" Theresa said disapprovingly to Nick. "Well, I suppose it's none of my business but I must say that- ." She broke off as Luke wandered out into the hallway to see who the visitor was.

"Never mind," she went on hastily. "Actually, I popped round because Fred's got no power. I was at his house and everything went off suddenly. So I thought I'd come and see whether your power is okay. Is it?"

"Yes, it's fine," Emma said. "I can hear the dishwasher running for a start."

"Then I suppose it's the fuse box," Theresa went on. "The trouble is, Fred doesn't seem to know where his fuse box is. Could one of you come and give me a hand?"

"I'll come," Nick said readily.

"I'll join you," Luke offered. "I may not be a great help, but you never know."

Left alone together, Emma and Penny looked at one another and smiled a little shyly.

"I don't suppose they'll be very long," Emma said reassuringly. "Shall I put the kettle on?"

"Yes, please – although it seems strange to be thinking about mundane things like cups of tea at a time like this," Penny replied, sounding slightly bemused.

"There's never a bad time to be thinking about a cup of tea!" Emma responded light-heartedly.

"Oh, Emma! I'm so happy!" Penny exclaimed joyously. "I can't believe Luke has asked me to marry him. Isn't it amazing? And I'm delighted for you and Nick too. I love a happy ending."

As she concluded, she seemed to think she might have been tactless. She coloured and said awkwardly, "I'm so sorry. I forgot. I didn't mean -."

"It's alright," Emma said quickly and encouragingly. "Sam was a Christian, so now he is in the best place of all – the supreme happy ending. We are so constrained by our mortal view of things and by what the world teaches us, that we tend to think of death as a tragedy but, for the believer, it's always the beginning of something so much better than this earthly life."

"You're very wise," Penny remarked wonderingly.

"I've had reason to reflect on it rather a lot."

"I suppose," Penny said doubtfully. "Can I ask – do you mind? How can you avoid making comparisons between Sam and Nick?"

"I don't know," Emma replied honestly. "I guess it's important not to dwell on any comparisons that come to mind – and never to voice them in a destructive way – or perhaps simply never to voice them! If it helps, I can tell you that at no time did I fall out of love with Nick – the real Nick. I only forced myself to try and forget him when he split up with me, because I was so badly hurt."

"If you hadn't really got over Nick, why did you marry Sam?" Penny asked impulsively. "I'm sorry –," she added hastily. "Don't answer that if you don't want to."

Emma reflected for a moment. "I don't mind," she said. "I met Sam at church in the autumn more than three years after Nick had broken up with me. I was so tired of being on my own – and, as far as I knew, there was no prospect of ever resolving things with Nick – or even wanting to, as I had no idea that there could be any excuse for his behaviour. Sam was so much in love with me and he was kind and decent. I decided that I would have to get on and make some kind of life for myself. I thought I could make Sam happy and I was grateful for his affection and his admiration. I hoped it was enough to build a marriage on – and it *was* a good marriage. We both worked hard to make it a good marriage – although sometimes I felt guilty about the fact that he was more in love with me than I was with him and, when he died, I blamed myself for having taken advantage of his love and for not having loved him more in return."

"While Nick and I were waiting to have a word with you after Sam's service, the man who was talking to you said that Sam had been very proud of you and very happy," Penny reminded her earnestly. "So I don't think you should feel bad on - on Sam's account."

"That's sweet of you."

There was a pause and then Penny asked, "Does Nick know all this?"

"We haven't spoken much about Sam but I'm sure we will. It isn't something to be rushed – both for Nick's sake and because it feels important to honour Sam's memory properly."

"Nick was shattered by your engagement to Sam," Penny confided. "He wouldn't speak about it much but it was obvious that he was really struggling – as much as in the months after he'd first broken up with you. He threw himself into his work and his church commitments and wore himself out so that he had as little time as possible to think."

"I'm sorry – I had no idea."

"Of course you didn't. We all knew that *you* couldn't be blamed in any way. When we watched him learn that he couldn't have children and then work through all the implications, we were heartbroken for him and so sorry for *you*. We thought he was doing the right - the honourable thing in letting you go, but it seemed such a tragedy for both of you."

"It was a *double* tragedy for him," Emma observed. "Losing the possibility of fatherhood at the same time as losing me. Goodness, that sounds conceited! Let's make that tea and talk about Luke instead."

Penny was very happy with the change of topic and the two girls sat for some time with their cups of tea and chatted about Luke and Penny's courtship, his work and his plans to move to London. Emma shared one or two reminiscences of her brother's earlier years and told Penny, with a twinkle, that their parents would be delighted with her.

"Mum was only saying last time she was here that she'd like him to find a nice Christian wife."

"I'm so glad he's a Christian," Penny acknowledged. "When he commented the first time we met that your church was rather different to the one he went to in Singapore, my ears pricked up. I thought he was fantastic, but I couldn't have gone out with him if he'd not been a Christian."

"He's never mentioned his church to me. Mind you, I've never asked. Did he say what makes it different?" Emma asked, her curiosity stirred.

"I think he was chiefly commenting on the age and style of the building."

"Did you know that later on the day he first met you he described you to me as 'a very pretty girl'?" Emma asked.

"How nice," Penny sighed and blushed.

"I've just remembered something," Emma went on ruefully. "When Luke told me he was seeing a girl here in the UK, I thought it would be difficult for him to sustain a relationship at such a distance; I feared it might lead to heartache and misunderstanding. Isn't that ironic? Nick and I have both been right here in the UK all along and our relationship has involved a lot more heartache and misunderstanding! I must learn not to be patronising."

Penny smiled, but remarked a little anxiously on the

extended absence of their two brothers. "Do you suppose everything's alright?"

"It *has* been a while," Emma conceded. "Perhaps they're just having difficulty tracking this fuse box down."

As she spoke the telephone rang; she lifted the receiver and found that, as she had almost anticipated, it was Luke on the line.

"Hi, Sis!" he said, sounding business-like. "No need to worry but Fred's been taken ill. We're waiting for an ambulance. We'll be back as soon as we can. I'll fill you in on the details then."

"Is there anything we can do?" Emma asked.

"Can't think of anything."

"Okay, but if something comes to mind, let us know."

"Right. Bye!"

The line went dead and Emma placed the receiver gently back on its stand, sending up a quick prayer for all those involved.

Emma hastily explained the situation to Penny, but the twins were beginning to stir so the girls went and collected them, carrying them downstairs and sitting at the kitchen table with a twin on each lap, before Emma filled Penny in on some of the background of her association with Theresa and Fred. Emma remarked that Theresa was likely to be upset at this turn of events, but when Luke and Nick eventually returned, she found that she had misjudged matters, for both young men commented on Theresa's ready acceptance of the situation.

"She was in a bit of a state to begin with, but once she'd got something positive to focus on, she was fine," Luke reported.

"She's packing up a bag for Fred and is planning to follow him up to the hospital with it once she's taken the dogs back to her house," Nick added. "She intends to look after Fred's dog while he's in hospital. We left her phoning Fred's son to let him know what's happened and she seems to think he'll give her a lift up to the hospital – but, if not, we told her to get in touch. We can always help out, if needed."

Emma agreed, offered to put the kettle back on and, once the twins were safely deposited in their playpen, demanded a fuller account of events.

It seemed that, having accompanied Theresa round to Fred's house, Nick and Luke had rung the doorbell several times without any answer; they had knocked and called – still no response. Theresa had pointed out early on that Fred was slow on his feet but she soon began to speculate that he had fallen asleep and might not hear them. As the two dogs were barking vigorously from inside, Luke had remarked that it would be surprising if anyone could sleep through such a commotion.

"That's when Theresa got in a bit of a flap," Luke recounted. "She was blaming herself for not having thought to take the key and asked us several times whether we could break the door down; but fortunately Nick spotted that one of the upstairs windows was open so he went off and borrowed a ladder from a neighbour and got in that way."

"Luckily, it was an old-fashioned sash window," Nick explained, as he and Luke accepted mugs of hot tea from Emma with a word of thanks. "So it was easy enough to push the lower part up out of the way and climb in, although it was rather disconcerting to see that we had collected several extra spectators by then."

Luke grinned. "You managed the manoeuvre with great panache," he remarked.

"Years of practice!" Nick joked.

"You'll have to watch this chap," Luke warned his sister facetiously.

Nick carried on with the tale, explaining that he had headed straight downstairs to look for Fred. "He was in his sitting room and he seemed to have fallen out of his chair - perhaps he'd been trying to get up. Anyway, I let Luke and Theresa in and, as we couldn't get any response from Fred, Luke phoned for an ambulance. They turned up pretty swiftly – and you know the rest."

"The paramedics were quite reassuring, but they wanted to get Fred to hospital as quickly as possible," Luke added. "While we were waiting for them to arrive Nick had dealt with the fuse box so, once the ambulance had gone, Theresa was perfectly happy to be left to sort things out at the house."

"And to look after Milo. She does love to be useful," Emma commented ruefully, but with genuine admiration for Theresa's spirit and her determination to be helpful.

"I clearly remember when I first met her here," Nick said reminiscently. "I think it was entirely thanks to her efforts to be 'useful' that you let me in the house at all!"

Emma grimaced and acknowledged that he had judged the matter very accurately, which allowed Luke to remind his sister of their mother's prediction that she would be glad of Theresa's help one day.

"How annoying that Mum should turn out to be right – although not, perhaps, in quite the way she envisaged!" Luke grinned.

The twins chose this moment to object to the lack of

adult attention and, as Nick moved to humour them, Luke remarked jocularly that Nick would have to get used to his new parental role rather speedily.

"Can't wait!" Nick replied cheerfully. "It'll be great to have a family – although apparently I have to take on the mother as well! I couldn't get the twins without her!"

When the laughter had subsided, Luke asked whether Nick had a date in mind for tying the knot.

"That's up to Emma," he replied.

"I'd like to talk to my vicar and his wife," Emma said. "They've been very kind and they might be able to give us some pointers as to when I shall have been widowed long enough for it to be considered acceptable to marry again. Not that it should be up to anyone else, but I don't want to cause too much gossip and indignation."

"'*Shall have been*,'" Luke repeated musingly. "What a great phrase. The future perfect tense – not used often enough, in my opinion. And that'll be my prayer for the two of you – that although your past was tense, your future together will be perfect! Of course, I realise that, as Christians, we each have a sure hope of a perfect future, but perhaps I can wish you both a foretaste of that perfection here and now."

CHAPTER 24

Nothing further was heard from Theresa during the course of the afternoon, but Nick and Penny were naturally more than happy to stay late and wait to see whether there was any news. Luke invited Penny to take a stroll round the garden so Nick and Emma tactfully stayed indoors, keeping an eye on the twins and enjoying their new-found understanding.

"I am so grateful to Luke and Penny," Nick remarked as he bounced Joel on his knee. "If they hadn't got together, I suppose you might never have agreed to listen to me."

Nick and Emma were seated side by side on the sofa in the front sitting room, Millie on Emma's lap and Joel on Nick's.

"Before I knew that Luke was seeing Penny," Emma replied. "I'd reached the point where I would have liked to ask you for some kind of explanation. I just didn't know how to begin when I'd sent you away with a flea in your ear."

"You were certainly pretty clear that day, after I kissed you," Nick said ruefully.

"I felt so guilty over Sam and so confused about what I thought of you. I'd made up my mind that you were untrustworthy, although your recent actions seemed to contradict that – but then there were some things that I just couldn't understand, couldn't excuse."

"Was that why you decided you needed to hear my side of things?"

"The first step was when I began to realise that Sam would have wanted me to be happy. He was a good man, Nick," Emma said earnestly.

"I know. Ed told me so a long time ago."

"How did that come up?" she asked, lifting Millie off her lap and sitting her on the floor by her feet with a few toys to hand.

"It was when he told me you were engaged to Sam," Nick said. "That was a real blow. I knew with the rational part of my mind that you would probably be no more lost to me married than you already were, but I couldn't treat it rationally. To think of you married to another man was – dreadful. I tried to tell myself that I was pleased you had recovered and moved on, but it wasn't true – I was devastated. I had always had in the back of my mind the distant possibility that, if you didn't marry, perhaps at some point I would have an opportunity to tell you what had happened and you might be willing to - to take me on after all. I hadn't reached any fixed conclusion about when that might be or how I might approach you, but your marriage to Sam rendered that hope futile."

"Except that, as things turned out, it didn't."

"Yes, but that leads to such a complex maze of guilt and joy, incomprehension and gratitude, that I've been trying to avoid thinking about it," Nick replied gravely. He put Joel down on the floor next to his sister as he spoke and, within seconds, Joel had deserted Millie and set off to explore.

"I know what you mean," Emma responded. "Penny and I touched on it earlier. Don't forget that Sam is with

God now and – and full of joy. I don't understand why things have worked out this way, but maybe we're not meant to understand. It can't be helpful to wonder whether God planned it like this – or – or why; but, as you pointed out, we can be sure that '*in all things God works for the good of those who love him*', so we should give thanks for his blessings and pray that, through our experiences, we'll be conformed more to the likeness of his Son – as it goes on to say in that passage – and then get on with living out our lives for him and not dwelling on unanswerable questions and regrets."

"I love you very much," Nick told her. "You're so sweet and sane and good. My feelings towards Sam and towards all that has happened have been so mixed: shock and self-reproach, relief and remorse, anger and doubt. I've been a mess. To begin with, I felt almost responsible for his death: I had resented him so much."

"Is that why you came to his service?" Emma asked, as enlightenment began to dawn.

"In part," he acknowledged, watching Joel head towards the gap between an armchair and the sofa. "I was very unsure about turning up, but I thought I owed it to him as a sort of apology. I had struggled not to begrudge him any happiness with you, but I had often failed. I suppose there was – still is – a sense of guilt or shame, perhaps, that I had disliked him for having what I – what I could not have; and then he had so little time to enjoy it. Inevitably, I knew my motives for going to the service were mixed because I was also impatient to see you again, so I asked my family what they thought I should do. They encouraged me to attend; my mother thought it might provide some sort of closure – and Penny offered to come with me in support."

"That was kind of her. I'm afraid I wasn't very friendly that day."

"No; but I understood that it was a very difficult occasion for you and that you had every reason to think badly of me." He paused. "At some point after that, did you wonder – begin to think that maybe I wasn't so bad, after all?"

Nick got to his feet as he spoke, and rescued Joel from the corner, putting him back on his hands and knees on the rug, but facing in a more sensible direction.

"Oh, you were so kind," Emma recalled. "So willing to help out when you called round. Of course it made me wonder about you. Charlie also made one or two comments which forced me to reconsider and, although I don't believe Ed has told her much, I thought that he'd have been less willing to continue to be your friend if you were as unscrupulous as I'd imagined over the years. Penny's visit also clarified something that I had – had misinterpreted," Emma finished bravely, knowing that Nick needed to know of her foolish mistake if he was to understand all her confusion, her doubts.

"What was that?"

"I discovered that Penny was your sister," Emma explained.

"I don't understand."

"I thought you were – um – living with Penny," Emma admitted reluctantly, hardly daring to meet Nick's eye for fear of derision.

"I am – oh, I *see*! *No*! That's ridiculous. When I brought Penny over to meet you after the service, I'm sure I said that I'd like to introduce you to one of my *sisters*."

"Did you? I didn't hear that – but I missed quite a lot of what happened that day. My brain wasn't functioning properly at all."

"So did you really think - ? Is that why you kept mentioning Penny and asking me whether she was okay with me visiting you?"

Emma nodded, very embarrassed, but Nick grinned widely.

"So when I kissed you, you must have thought I was some kind of Lothario! No wonder you reacted with such outrage."

"I was in a complete a muddle."

"That makes two of us," Nick acknowledged. "I was torn between wanting to justify myself to you and feeling that I should wait and respect your very natural wish to grieve for Sam. I shouldn't have kissed you that day. It was a stupid thing to do, when I'd not even begun to give you any kind of explanation. Afterwards, I couldn't believe I'd been such an idiot. And when I thought that I might have completely thrown away any chance of ever redeeming myself in your eyes, I was furious with myself – and desperate. I considered writing to you – in fact, I tried to put it all down on one occasion, but it sounded so pompous that I tore it up. I was thinking of asking Ed to try and arrange for us to meet again by some means, but I wasn't sure how to go about it and I still doubted whether I could persuade you to listen to me."

"It would have worked out somehow, don't you think?" Emma said reassuringly. "Looking back, it seems as if this was meant to happen – ever since we met again in the spring."

Nick smiled affectionately at her certainty.

"So did Ed know about you – about your situation all along?" Emma wanted to know.

"Not at all. I thought it best not to give him any kind of explanation at the time because there was a risk of it getting back to you via Charlie. But when he told me – very casually – about your engagement to Sam, he saw how shaken I was and he asked me directly whether I still cared. I'd given myself away pretty completely so I admitted it and, of course, he tore me off a strip or two for having behaved so badly to you. I was so miserable that I told him the truth. I thought it wouldn't make a difference to you any more if you did hear something, but I swore him to secrecy anyway and it seems as though he's kept his promise."

"Yes, Charlie didn't seem to know much. I've been wanting to ask," Emma went on. "Did you never in the last six years think of asking someone else out?"

"Never. I was still in love with you, so how could I begin to consider anyone else? I had given you every reason to think badly of me, but *I* had absolutely no reason to think badly of you. I knew I had lost a prize of great worth."

Emma blushed, disclaimed and hastened to say: "And what did you think that day when I turned up at Charlie's house?"

"Initially, it was just appallingly painful; but almost immediately I became more concerned for you than for me. I could see that you were in some distress. When I asked after Sam and you told me he'd died, I felt only shock and – and anxiety on your behalf. I could hardly bear to think of you coping alone with your loss and with two small babies. All other thoughts were suspended while I was with you.

Later, when I was able to reflect on your visit, I started to try and think of ways to help you and then I began to realise that you were widowed and to consider what that might mean for me – to comprehend that you were free again and that there might be a second chance for me eventually, if you recovered from your bereavement and I could persuade you to forgive me – and if you were willing to look at a man who – who couldn't give you any more children."

"Oh, hush!" said Emma gently.

"I should have asked how you feel about that. Will you mind very much?"

"I love you," Emma told him with complete conviction. "That's all that matters. Besides, I *have* two children. We have a wonderful family to raise together."

"Are you sure, my darling? Are you really sure?"

"Yes, of *course*," she replied indignantly.

"But have you really thought about it?" he urged.

"Have *you* thought about it?"

"I've had six years to get used to the idea."

"No, I meant - have you thought about all the implications of marrying *me?*"

"Yes, I shall be the happiest man alive – happier than I ever thought to be."

"But, in the words of my brother-in-law, you'll be saddling yourself with another chap's babies. Apparently, no one's going to be keen to take on that kind of responsibility. My sister's advice was not to set my sights too high – maybe settle for a widower or some divorced chap."

"Perhaps she'd think my circumstances would count equally poorly in the marriage stakes," Nick suggested. "Anyway, to me the twins are an amazing bonus. As you said, I'm acquiring a fantastic, ready-made family – a family I'd assumed I could never have. It will be a huge privilege to help look after them."

Millie, who had been attempting to reach an interesting toy that was just beyond the stretch of her small arm, chose that moment to set up a howl of frustration and Nick laughed in a wonderfully carefree way at the impeccable timing and gathered her and the toy up, one in each hand, and sat Millie on the sofa between himself and Emma, passing Millie the toy and telling her fondly that she would have to master the art of crawling if she was going to set her heart on things that were out of reach.

Mille chuckled uncomprehendingly but cheerfully at him and then devoted her attention to her newly acquired plaything.

"Amidst her other, more suspect advice, my sister did tell me that the twins need a father figure!" Emma remarked with amusement. "And I've just remembered some words which came to mind the night after I met you again in the spring – just a couple of days after Sam's death. It was the phrase: 'I will not leave you as orphans.' The Lord keeps his promises in the most unexpected ways and often at more than one level."

"Amen to that," said Nick.

"I wonder how Rachel will react to news of our engagement," Emma went on musingly. "And others too. There are bound to be some who don't know or don't care about the circumstances, who will just be shocked at our apparent hurry."

"Your idea of speaking to your vicar is a good one," Nick replied.

"I suppose we should just do what we decide is right and not fret about other people's opinions. Luke was saying that yesterday."

"He's right - except, I guess, where our actions and decisions have an impact on other people's faith."

"That makes it more complicated. How can we tell?"

"By praying?" Nick suggested. "By using our common sense; by asking for advice? We'll work it out together," he added.

"Together," Emma repeated with satisfaction. "I like the sound of that."

CHAPTER 25

Nick and Emma were to be given an early opportunity to hear one person's opinion of their relationship.

Theresa contacted Emma after tea to express her gratitude for all the assistance she had received that afternoon. "Your brother and that friend of yours – Nicholas, is it? – were very obliging; and very ready with offers of additional help. I won't need to trouble any of you at the moment, dear, because it seems as though Fred is likely to be kept in hospital for several days at least, but I did appreciate the offers, so do tell them."

Emma assured her that she would pass on her thanks and, having enquired after Fred's condition in more detail, thought that the conversation was nearing its conclusion, but she found that Theresa had more to say.

"That Nicholas – is that his name?"

Emma agreed warily that it was.

"That Nicholas – now my advice is…" Theresa paused impressively. "Ask him to make an honest woman of you."

There was stunned silence for a moment and then Emma began to laugh helplessly.

"There's no need to react like that," Theresa remonstrated, very much on her dignity. "It's a perfectly sensible suggestion. Nicholas is a pleasant young man and he's plainly interested in you or I wouldn't keep meeting him at your house. Also, you need to find someone to help bring up those twins of yours – and the sooner the better."

When she could speak, and with the laughter still clear in her voice, Emma replied, "I agree – *we* agree. In fact, we agree so wholeheartedly that Nick and I got engaged this afternoon."

"Engaged?" Theresa repeated sharply.

"Unofficially," Emma confirmed, wondering what Theresa would say next.

"Well done, dear," she responded heartily, surprising Emma again. "That's a piece of good news to put against today's bad news and I think it's very wise of you. If I were you, I'd set an early date for the wedding and get things regularised."

Emma was not especially enamoured of the assumption that anything needed to be regularised, but as Theresa had reacted in an unexpectedly uncritical way to the news, she did not cavil.

She enjoyed relaying the gist of the conversation to her companions, although she remarked that there was something about the way Theresa delivered her advice that made it seem quite appealing to run entirely counter to everything she suggested.

"Oh dear!" Nick exclaimed, in mock dismay.

"It's alright," Luke joked. "Just bribe Theresa to tell Emma that she always recommends very long engagements!"

Luke did not wish to publicise his own engagement while his job situation was still unsettled, although he understood that Penny was eager to tell her family and did not object to the news being spread thus far, while remaining firm in his determination not to share it with his own circle for the time being. In fact, he said that he had no intention of telling his parents until he was safely settled in a job in London, so that they could not imagine they could influence his plans in any way.

By contrast, Nick and Emma were agreed that, between them, they would inform all their family and friends of their plans at the earliest opportunity. They were both keen to make their situation known so that acquaintances could begin to grow accustomed to the notion.

Emma was not particularly sanguine about her parents' reaction. Both her father and mother were people of set ideas and she thought their opinion of Nick was likely to be based uncompromisingly on their knowledge of his former behaviour. She had wondered whether Luke's news might deflect their attention a little but, with that distraction vetoed, she had little doubt that she would come under the full force of their disapprobation. However, the conversation had to take place and so, after breakfast on Monday morning, when Luke had headed into London, she mustered her thoughts and her courage and phoned the Nepalese hospital where her parents worked, intending to catch them in their lunchbreak, as that was the time when they usually phoned her.

When she was advised that neither Dr George nor Dr Dorothy Mann was available, she was not sure whether to be relieved or disappointed. She left a message asking them to call when they could but making it clear that there was no emergency and, assuming that she would hear from them at the end of their working day, took the twins out to the local shops to make various purchases.

It had been arranged that, as Luke was booked on an early flight back to Singapore on Tuesday morning, he and Penny would meet in London after work on Monday so they could spend the evening together, dining in town and making the most of the short time Luke had left in the UK. Meanwhile, Nick was to visit Emma again on Monday evening, bringing with him a takeaway meal of some kind, and Emma had offered to provide a dessert and wanted to acquire some fresh ingredients.

Returning home contentedly with her shopping and anticipating a pleasant evening, Emma found that there was a message on her answerphone and pressed the button to listen to it as she lifted the twins out of the pushchair.

"Emma," came her father's abrupt voice. "Are you there? What is the point of asking us to call and then not answering the phone? Call us!"

Instantly, Emma's mood of gentle euphoria was deflated and as she dialled her parents' number again she was already nervous and on the defensive.

This time, her mother answered the phone and immediately asked whether Emma had had any contact with her brother lately. Fortunately, she did not wait for an answer but went on to inform her daughter that they had tried to call him a couple of times over the weekend without success. "Do you know where he is?" she demanded.

"No," Emma replied reluctantly, consoling herself with the thought that it was the exact truth after all and knowing that Luke would not want to be cross-questioned.

"If you hear from him, tell him we want to speak to him," her mother said. "He's really very poor at keeping in touch. Now, what was it you were calling about?"

Already flustered from feeling obliged to answer her mother disingenuously, Emma replied without thinking. "I'm engaged!" she blurted out.

"You're *what?*"

"I'm engaged."

"To whom?"

"Nick Knight," Emma confessed.

"*Nick Knight!*" her mother repeated heatedly. "Why on earth would you do that?"

"Because we met again and we still love each other. It was all a – a misunderstanding, when we split up before."

"That's ridiculous! Sam has only been dead for a few months. What are you thinking of? It is far too soon. You know, in Nepal, widows traditionally have no rights. They are often shunned and they are *certainly* not permitted to remarry."

In the background, Emma could hear her father demanding an explanation. Her mother enlightened him.

"*Nick Knight!*" he thundered. "Let me speak to her!"

The receiver was handed over.

"For God's sake, Emma, don't be a fool!" he barked down the line at her. "After he behaved so badly last time, why would you get entangled with him again? Leopards never change their spots!"

"Nick had good reasons for the way he behaved."

"Did he make any attempt to explain at the time?"

"No, but –"

"Then you can't trust him. Communication is the only foundation for a healthy marriage."

"The *only* foundation?" she queried.

"It is absolutely essential," he insisted, emphasising each syllable.

"The – the circumstances were exceptional," Emma defended Nick.

"Hmph! It seems as though he knows how to win you over at any rate. But if you don't learn from your mistakes, you'll never learn anything," her father told her - a statement which was as manifestly untrue as it was unkind.

"It was not a mistake!" Emma objected. "Nick was –"

But her father gave her no chance to explain.

"If your heart is set on being jilted all over again, I suppose we can't stop you!" he interjected and hung up without any parting valediction, leaving Emma hurt but unsurprised, and wondering how best to take things forward. A short period of quiet reflection and prayer did much to restore her equilibrium and she put her regrets aside until she could share the problem with Nick later.

Charlie unexpectedly dropped in on her friend during the afternoon, bringing little Dan with her and plainly brimming with news. Emma immediately invited them in and before they had even reached the kitchen, Charlie announced that Ed had heard from Nick's company that morning, and they had offered him a job.

"Wonderful! Will he accept it?" Emma asked.

"He already has."

"Good gracious!"

"I know, but he told me after the interview that, if they wanted him, he'd accept," Charlie explained.

Emma was delighted at this turn of events and eager to hear more, so, as the weather was dry and warm, they carried a couple of rugs out into the back garden and spread them out on the lawn, provided toys for the youngsters and drinks for the adults, and sat out in the sunshine to discuss developments and to agree that Ed's relaxed nature and his intelligence would enable him to adapt quickly to a new environment.

Dan soon wandered off and found some twigs and pebbles to play with, but the twins required closer attention and Joel had to be repeatedly collected from explorations that took him off the rugs and across the grass.

When Ed's work situation had been fully reviewed, Emma began to consider telling Charlie about her engagement to Nick, although she felt extraordinarily shy about introducing the topic, particularly after her parents' unfavourable response. Millie's attention was concentrated on a musical toy and she seemed happily occupied, but Emma was obliged to rescue Joel from another bid for freedom. She seated him in her lap and showed him a book, but he rejected it with every evidence of loathing and wriggled to escape, protesting vehemently at the restriction to his freedom of movement.

"Perhaps we should go indoors?" Emma suggested.

"No, wait there!" Charlie commanded, getting to her feet.

Emma looked at her friend in surprise at her unusually dictatorial tone.

"I'll be back in a moment," Charlie said and headed indoors. She reappeared a few moments later with the playpen and set it down on the grass next to the rugs with a slight thump.

"Now put Joel in there. He'll be fine for a bit. I think

you've got some news to share as well," Charlie remarked meaningfully.

"Oh!" Emma exclaimed self-consciously. "I suppose Ed's already spoken to Nick." She lifted Joel into the playpen, which contained a selection of toys, and he condescended to investigate.

"Of course he has!" Charlie replied. "He rang him to let him know about the job offer and to thank him for his help. And Nick just happened to mention a little piece of news that he thought might be of interest! I suppose it didn't occur to you to tell me?"

"I was just about to," Emma defended herself. "I was trying to work out how to start."

"Mmm. I don't know whether I believe you! You will have to make up for it by giving me *all* the details. Come on now!"

"If Nick has told Ed, there's not much more I can add," Emma replied, demurely playful.

"Oh, you know what men are like," Charlie said, with a dismissive wave of her hand. "They exchange the basic information – if they happen to think of it – but there's never any detail. I don't suppose it even occurred to Ed to ask how it all came about, despite the fact that, as far as we knew, you and Nick were barely on speaking terms! So, spill the beans!"

Emma smiled at her friend's imperious eagerness but said mischievously that she thought the twins might need changing.

"Not a chance! You're not getting off this rug till you've told me everything. And if I have to sit on you, I think we both know you'll regret it!"

So Emma outlined the happenings of the previous day and found that there was great joy in being able to clear Nick's name completely and explain the motivation for his past actions.

Charlie's exuberant amazement at the explanation and at the latest developments was increased by the satisfaction of having her more recent estimation of Nick's character confirmed and her husband's friendship vindicated, and by the pleasure of anticipating Emma's future happiness and all the benefits which would accrue to the twins from growing up in a stable family with two parents.

It was a day for great rejoicing and the two friends chatted and prayed together for as long as their offspring permitted. Amidst the other and greater causes for rejoicing, both Emma and Charlie expressed their appreciation for their mutual friendship and the help and encouragement it had brought over the years. Emma pointed out that her friendship with Charlie had led to both her initial encounter with Nick and the more recent renewal of their acquaintance.

"I had no idea I could be so influential!" Charlie laughed. "I expect to be matron of honour at your wedding, at the very least – although I'd rather not be pregnant at the time. When are you planning to get married?"

"I don't know. I'll speak to Michael about it and see how he reacts. Not everyone will be as positive as you."

Emma went on to share something of the way her parents had received the news of her engagement and her hurt was a little eased by Charlie's ready sympathy and partisan support.

"Don't worry about it," she advised sturdily. "You don't need their permission."

"I know, but I'd like to feel that they weren't completely opposed to our plans. I'd like them to value Nick as I do."

"They'll come round," Charlie predicted comfortably. "They just need a bit of time."

Emma thought they would need more than time; they would need to hear Nick's side of the story. In other circumstances, she would have asked Luke to try to explain things to them but, since Luke had made it clear that he had no intention of contacting his parents at the moment, that option was not open to her.

Charlie eventually said that she and Dan ought to be going, so Emma carried the twins inside and stood at the front door with her arms full to watch them depart. She had been so very blessed in her friendship with Charlie and she looked forward to many more years of close companionship, particularly as Nick and Ed were also friends and would now be work colleagues. She hoped that in the future she would be able to repay some of Charlie's many kindnesses.

CHAPTER 26

In credit to his eagerness, Nick arrived promptly that evening and Emma was relieved to learn that his family had reacted much more positively to the news of their engagement than her own parents. Nick reported that his mother and father and all seven of his other siblings and half-siblings were overjoyed and were longing to meet Emma at last and welcome her into their large family. His parents were already working out how soon they could get down from Berwick-on-Tweed to London and when they could invite Emma and Nick up to the North of England, where most of the family were based.

On being informed of the sadly adverse reaction of Emma's parents, Nick said mildly that they would naturally be concerned to ascertain that their daughter was not taking a step she would regret. "It's different for my family. They were fully in the picture in the first place and are just glad that I've got a second chance. I suppose it'll take a while for your parents to come round to the idea that I'm not a nasty piece of work who ditched their daughter without a second thought."

"That's what Charlie said - but Dad was so angry that I had no chance to explain anything, so how are they ever going to hear the truth about you?" Emma replied, downcast.

"Perhaps we should do what I considered doing when you wouldn't listen to me," Nick suggested. "Perhaps we should send them a letter – or an email. Would they read it, do you suppose?"

Emma rather thought that curiosity would compel them to read it – curiosity and a desire to defend the accuracy of their own position. So, once the twins were asleep for the night, Nick and Emma drafted an email to her parents, setting out as concisely as possible the events of six years previously.

Sending it off, Emma prayed that they would read it and would change their minds, but she tried not to dwell on it, for she had never seen her parents back down from a strongly held position and she rather thought they would prefer to follow the inflexible example of Sergius Saranoff, who famously insisted that he would never apologise.

Luke returned home at bedtime very pleased with the outcome of his day in London. He had secured an assurance that he would be welcome to transfer there from the Singapore office and that it should take only a couple of months for the move to be organised. Accordingly, he departed for the airport on the first leg of his journey back to Singapore the next morning, in as good a mood as can be expected from a young man faced with the prospect of being separated from his fiancée for several weeks.

Once he had gone, Emma picked up the phone and made an appointment to see her vicar later in the day. Michael offered to call on Emma and brought his wife to the meeting, and Emma soon learnt that Theresa had not kept her information to herself but had already spread the news of her engagement to a number in the church family.

Emma sensed that Michael and Janet were shocked and doubtful about this development, but they kept their own counsel and wisely invited her to explain. They listened with interest to an outline of the history of her relationship with Nick, and began to comprehend the situation better and to be more encouraging.

Michael sensibly suggested that he and Janet should meet Nick as soon as possible, so Emma invited them all round for lunch the following Saturday. The gathering passed off very well. Michael and Janet were able to have a long chat with Nick and to see him interacting with Emma and the twins, and Emma rejoiced in the certainty that everything he said and did demonstrated his kindness and his integrity. She thought it only as she should have anticipated that, at the end of the get-together, Michael and Janet gave the prospective union their blessing and indicated that they would be happy to agree to a wedding sometime the following year. Michael concluded by reading with them Psalm Sixty-Eight and directing them in particular to verses four to six:

> *Sing to God, sing in praise of his name,*
> *extol him who rides on the clouds; rejoice*
> *before him - his name is the Lord.*
> *A father to the fatherless, a defender of*
> *widows, is God in his holy dwelling.*
> *God sets the lonely in families.*

Even with Luke's prohibition on the disclosure of his plans, there was plenty for Rachel to exclaim over on her return from the family holiday in Florida. Emma, who had not heard anything further from her parents, was so relieved to find that her sister welcomed the news of her engagement to Nick, that she was able to overlook the suspicion that some of Rachel's pleasure sprang from a desire to see Emma respectably settled and taken care of without any effort on Rachel's part and some from a general sense of satisfaction at imagining that Emma had followed her good advice in seeking out a father for the twins.

Rachel also had a great deal to tell her sister about her trip to Florida – about the superb food they had eaten, the splendid hotel in which they had stayed and the amazing luxury of the whole trip, but Emma registered only one thing as particularly noteworthy and somewhat amusing. Rachel had apparently struck up a friendship with an American family staying at the same hotel, and especially with the mother, Grace.

"Very rich, Emma – and I mean *very* rich!" Rachel informed her sister impressively. "Family money; and Holden - the husband - has a job that must pay millions of dollars a year. He took Harry out for a couple of rounds of golf and they got on really well – I knew his golf would come in useful one day. It sounds as though they have the most amazing house. And they're planning to visit England next summer so we'll all meet up again then. It turns out they're Christians – 'born again' – you know the kind of thing – and Grace has asked me to recommend a good church in London. Harry is going to go to this meeting in a few weeks' time and ask his CEO whether he can suggest something suitable – maybe even his own church. What an opportunity for Harry to get noticed by his CEO. It's as if it was all meant to be."

Emma, who was sure it was 'all meant to be', smiled to herself and shared the tale with Nick at the first opportunity. Amongst many other petitions, they prayed together for God to continue to be at work in the lives of Rachel and her family, and so they were pleased but not unduly surprised to learn, in the course of time, that Harry's presence at the event in September led to his attendance at a number of other such meetings, that Tilly had been allowed to go to church with her friend, Bea, and that Rachel had also begun to attend her local church occasionally. From such small beginnings, God could surely work great miracles.

Although Fred's stay in hospital was of considerable duration, he did eventually make a gradual recovery and was able to return to his own home some weeks later. Theresa, who had visited him assiduously in hospital, taking idiosyncratic offerings of food and reports of Milo, went on visiting him at home and, after a while, moved in with him to be his full-time carer. This seemed to suit everyone, although there were times when Emma thought the benefits to Fred dearly bought by her at the price of frequent conversations initiated by Theresa through the hedge at the foot of her garden. She also wondered, with a wry smile, whether Theresa had given any thought to the neighbours' assumptions in this instance.

As the months passed, it became apparent that Emma's parents had accepted the inevitability of her wedding and, moreover, that they intended to be there to witness it, but it was just as well that Emma had not allowed herself to hope for any kind of retraction or apology from them, since they did not once refer to her email or express any kind of regret at their initial refusal to countenance the match. When

Emma endeavoured to press them, they rose sublimely above all debate.

Nick and Emma fixed on a wedding date in late April, which would be after the first anniversary of Sam's death and, as Charlie's baby was due in February, should ensure that she would be able to act as matron of honour at the ceremony, as she had light-heartedly requested. In recognition of his own invaluable role in bringing Emma and Nick together, Nick invited Ed to be his best man, a role which he very gladly accepted. Dan was rather too young to be given a formal part in proceedings and, of course, there would be the new baby to consider, but Charlie's parents pronounced themselves to be very happy to take charge of their grandchildren for the duration.

Once Luke had made the move from Singapore to London, he and Penny began to think about setting a date for their own wedding and making their engagement more widely known. Luke's parents were undoubtedly surprised at the news but raised no major objections to the marriage, although his mother seemed less pleased at the prospect than one might have expected had one heard her views, as formerly expressed to Emma, on the benefits of Luke finding a 'nice Christian girl' with whom to settle down.

Setting aside a little disappointment that she could not make capital amongst her circle of acquaintance from either the achievements or social standing of Luke's fiancée, Rachel was in general rather pleased to find that her brother intended to tie the knot and she consoled herself for her disappointment with the reflection that it would not have been particularly pleasant to be required to cede her pre-eminent, familial position of success and financial stability to her brother and his wife, had Penny been richer, better connected or more successful.

Moreover, she was able to congratulate herself on the fact that she and Harry were doing very nicely and were beginning to establish friendships with some rather influential people. Their new American friends were certainly worth cultivating. Harry had found that his CEO knew of the family and, as a result, had secured the promise of an invitation to lunch at his CEO's country house when Holden and Grace came over to England in the summer.

With such prospects for happiness before her, Rachel listened with tolerable equanimity to the revelation that Nick was contemplating going into the church in a year or two's time. She would have greatly preferred Nick to realise sudden fame or success in a more worldly arena which she could drop casually into conversation with her friends, but she supposed he might eventually attain some degree of eminence by being made an archdeacon or a bishop or something of the kind. It must be hoped that, before she realises the disappointment of her hopes in that regard, she will learn that God's view of temporal hierarchies is rather different to hers.

Nick and Emma were untroubled by worldly ambitions. Nick was clear that he felt God's calling and simply wanted to be sure that he had Emma's support, that he was not being unfair to the twins and that he was doing the right thing by his current employers. As for Emma, she was blissfully happy. This was the future she had envisaged for them both when she had first known Nick, and now, after all the heartache of the intervening years, it was to be a reality. "Through all the difficulties '*The Lord was my support*,'" she said. "*He brought me out into a spacious place.*" Truly, she and Nick could affirm that they had seen '*the goodness of the Lord in the land of the living*'. Their future together would be built on that conviction, and they were ever sensible of great gratitude to God and of the huge debt they owed to Sam, whose children brightened all their days.

Lightning Source UK Ltd.
Milton Keynes UK
UKHW012226030519
342082UK00001B/6/P